Tales from Grace Chapel Inn®

They Also Serve

Pam Hanson & Barbara Andrews

Guideposts

NEW YORK, NEW YORK

They Also Serve

ISBN-13: 978-0-8249-4761-3

Published by Guideposts
16 East 34th Street
New York, New York 10016
www.guideposts.com

Distributed by Ideals Publications
2636 Elm Hill Pike, Suite 120
Nashville, Tennessee 37214

Library of Congress Cataloging-in-Publication Data has been applied for.

Cover by Lookout Design Group
Interior design by Cindy LaBreacht
Typeset by Nancy Tardi

Printed and bound in the United States of America

10 9 8 7 6 5 4 3 2 1

# Acknowledgments

To Leo Grant and everyone at Guideposts who made writing this book such a pleasure.

—Pam Hanson and Barbara Andrews

Chapter One

Raindrops danced on the walkway to Grace Chapel Inn Saturday morning as Alice Howard stepped out the front door onto the long front porch. She pulled up the hood on her yellow rain jacket and opened her cherry red umbrella. *What a sight I must be.* She smiled, garbed from head to toe in bright primary colors. She stomped her feet to get the feel of her sister Jane's red gardening boots, then started down the steps.

She felt as though God was giving the earth a good spring cleaning, washing away the last of the winter grime with a warm April shower. What a blessing it was to have a friend like Vera who thought it was good fun to walk in the rain. Alice was on her way to their meeting place at Fred's Hardware, the business Vera's husband operated. It made a good starting place for a nice long walk.

Alice splashed down the steps and through the shallow pools that had accumulated in front of the inn after several rainy days. She was reminded of the fun she'd had as a child wading through mud puddles until her boots filled with water.

The rain plopping on her umbrella had a rhythm of its own, and she couldn't help humming along. Words of a favorite hymn went through her head:

"Joyful, joyful, we adore Thee, God of glory, Lord of love."

She could imagine Beethoven writing the original music for this wonderful hymn on just such a day as this. Of course, she was being fanciful, but she kept humming:

"Giver of immortal gladness, fill us with the light of day."

She didn't remember the words to the second verse, but she continued making soft music as she splashed along, her heart filled with joy. Indeed, she had many reasons to be thankful. The bed-and-breakfast was prospering, allowing the three Howard sisters to live in their late father's home and share the work of running it. Alice loved her job as a nurse at the Potterston Hospital and took great pleasure in her friends and other interests. But, of course, the very core of her existence was her faith in the Lord. He had never failed her.

She remembered the end of the third verse and sang under her breath:

"Lift us to the joy divine."

Ahead she could see Vera walking toward her through the curtain of rain. When they were a few yards apart, they both stopped and broke out laughing. They were practically mirror images of each other. Alice was a bit taller and thinner than Vera, but both were wearing bright yellow rain gear and old-fashioned rubber boots. Vera's umbrella had red and green stripes, and she wore a matching rain hat instead of a hood. Otherwise they were almost twins.

"It looks like we were thinking alike," Alice said.

"I'm glad you talked me into walking in the rain," Vera said. "I splashed through puddles all the way here. You would think I was an elementary school student instead of a teacher."

"I don't recall having to persuade you. Fred must think we're loony."

"No, my husband knows us better than that. In fact, I

think he's a bit envious. We get to play in the rain, and he has to open the store. Usually Saturday morning is busy. All the weekend carpenters and gardeners come in for last minute supplies."

"Where should we walk?"

"Oh, let's circle the town and then head down Village Road if the visibility isn't too bad. I'm willing to dodge raindrops, but I don't want cars sneaking up behind me."

"I love walking in the country on days when the fog is still covering the valleys like a fluffy down quilt," Alice said.

"You love everything in and around Acorn Hill," Vera said, her lively blue eyes flashing with good humor. "That's why it's so much fun to walk with you. Part of me will be glad when school is out for summer break. We'll be able to walk more often."

At sixty-two, Alice was ten years older than her companion. They had met when Vera was engaged to marry Fred Humbert and became fast friends. Besides their walks, they shared a love of reading, especially cozy mysteries. In fact, Vera still liked to curl up with a Nancy Drew once in a while. It reminded her of the kind of story her fifth-grade girls liked to read.

Alice headed down Chapel Road with Vera by her side, their umbrellas so close they swished together as they walked. "I love the look of wet brick," Alice commented as they got to the corner. The volunteer fire department kept the town's engine in a squat brick building with two big overhead doors. "Even old buildings look new."

"Oh, look, Viola is just opening Nine Lives." Vera called out to the owner of the town's only bookstore, "Good morning, Viola."

"My, I didn't expect anyone to be out this morning," Viola said as they approached. "If it keeps raining like this, we'll need to build an ark."

She started to open the front door of her shop, giving herself an impatient shake to shed some of the rain clinging to her long blue raincoat.

"We're having a great time splashing through puddles," Alice assured her.

"Step inside for a minute. There's something I want to ask you." Viola removed the plastic rain bonnet that covered her cropped steel-gray hair and gave it a good shake as they entered the store.

"It's just a quick question, really," the bookstore owner said, hovering in the open doorway. "I need to talk to Louise as soon as possible, but I don't want to interrupt if she's busy with piano students this morning. Can you suggest a good time to call?"

"Let me think," Alice said, trying to remember her older sister's schedule for the morning. "She mentioned an early makeup lesson for one of her pupils who's been ill. They're probably in the middle of that right now. Other than that, I think she only has one other before she's free. She mentioned wanting to spend the rest of the morning catching up on the inn's books. Jane and I are so lucky that she enjoys accounting. We're both hopeless when it comes to balancing our finances. They can be so complicated, even for a small business like ours. But, of course, you know that from running your store."

"I'll give her a call in an hour or so," Viola said, sounding unusually distracted. "Thank you, Alice. Enjoy your walk, ladies."

"That was a bit strange," Vera said as they continued down Berry Lane past the town hall. "It's almost impossible to have even a short conversation with Viola without some mention of literature."

"She didn't seem quite herself this morning," Alice agreed. "She must have something important on her mind."

"Usually it's impossible to pass her store without being invited inside for tea and book talk. Not that I don't enjoy it. It gives me a chance to discuss with her the latest and best children's books. It's so important to start children early with a love of reading."

They were passing Time for Tea, a little shop on the corner of Berry Lane and Acorn Avenue.

"I hate to admit it," Vera said, "but I'm about ready for a rest stop. This rain slicker is awfully warm. I only thought of keeping dry when I put it on, but it's better suited to cooler temperatures."

"I'm a bit overheated too," Alice agreed, "but let's keep going. If we make a full circle of the town, we can stop at the Coffee Shop on our way home."

They looked both ways as they crossed Acorn Avenue heading east to Village Road. The rain dripping off their umbrellas made poor visibility, but they had the streets virtually to themselves in the continuing deluge.

"The rain has certainly kept people inside," Vera commented. "This isn't the bustling town I'm used to on Saturday morning. Maybe this would be a good time to stop at Clip 'n' Curl to make a hair appointment. I need a cut before I take my class on their field trip."

"Where are you—" Alice's words were drowned out by a tremendous rumble.

"Goodness! I wasn't expecting thunder and lightning," Vera said. "That sounded awfully close."

"Let's cut through the alley and the town parking lot." Alice led the way to a shortcut that would bring them back to Hill Street as another loud burst of thunder warned them off the streets.

They hustled down an alley, then through the town lot half filled with cars and pickup trucks. In a minute they were in front of the Coffee Shop.

Leaning into the wind brought by the sudden storm, Alice led the way, pausing only to close the umbrella and shake out the water before going inside.

Inclement weather hadn't discouraged many of the shop's regulars, and several booths were occupied. Vera led the way past the counter, where treats baked by the local bakery were displayed under plastic domes.

"It takes a stronger woman than I to walk past these goodies without wanting one," Vera joked as she paused to look at a luscious assortment of bear claws, Danish pastries and muffins.

They made their way to a back corner, pausing to greet neighbors and friends as they went. The Coffee Shop was a breakfast club for many local residents, especially on a Saturday morning, when farm families came into town to shop. As though to confirm that they'd made a wise decision to seek shelter, a brilliant bolt of lightning lit up the sky outside the large front window.

Alice smiled at Samuel Bellwood and asked about his family, then watched as he made his way through the shop, stopping to visit at several other booths. Leaving the Coffee Shop could take a good bit of time, she knew, but no doubt the sheep farmer was in no hurry to brave the storm outside.

"Ah, it's good to get out of this slicker," Vera said, hanging it on a peg on the wall before she slid onto a booth seat.

Alice hung up her jacket and put her wet umbrella on a crowded rubber mat. June Carter, the shop's owner, waved a greeting from behind the counter as she filled a coffee pot from a big urn.

"I'll be with you in a minute," she called out. "Hope's car wouldn't start this morning, so I'm all alone. When it rains it pours, or so they say."

"No hurry at all, June," Alice said to the pleasant, middle-aged woman who was also a member of the board at Grace

Chapel, the church where Alice's father had served as minister for many years. "We're just taking shelter from the storm."

"It sure did get nasty fast," June said, continuing to refill coffee cups to a chorus of agreement from her customers.

"Well, this is a perfect example of the lemonade principle," Vera said with a soft laugh.

"What's that?" Alice asked.

"When God gives you a lemon—that's the thunderstorm that ruined our walk—make lemonade. Or in this case, have a nice morning snack. We can't take up June's booth space without ordering something."

Alice laughed, knowing that her slightly plump friend fought a good battle against weight gain most of the time, but she was more than willing to transgress when the opportunity presented itself.

"What can I get you ladies?" June asked, automatically putting empty cups in front of both of them, then filling Vera's to the brim with steaming coffee. She had a genius for remembering people's tastes, and she knew what both women would want to drink.

"Tea, of course," Alice said, knowing June would bring a pot of hot water and an assortment of flavors in a woven basket lined with a linen napkin. "And I'll have a lemon–poppy seed muffin if you have one left."

"Sure do," June said with no need to check her stock.

"A cheese Danish," Vera said with just a trace of guilty pleasure in her voice. "I haven't had one in ages."

"Coming up," June said as she hurried away.

"You didn't get a chance to tell me where you're taking your class on the field trip," Alice reminded her as they waited for their order.

"Philadelphia. I'm really excited! There's so much to do there, and my fifth graders are a bright group. They're ready to soak up the history of our country's founding. They've worked hard all year on little fundraising projects like selling candy, so we'll be able to have a really nice lunch at no expense to parents. We'll leave very early in the morning and have a full day for sightseeing and fun."

"When are you leaving?"

"April 30, a week from Monday. You'd be amazed at how many details there are in planning a school trip. At least I have enough chaperones. The school is very strict about that, but my parents have been good about volunteering this year. The trick is to find ones who don't have to work on a week-day. Very few of my students have stay-at-home mothers these days. I lucked out in getting my quota for the trip."

"How does a trip like that work? Do you have to make reservations for the places you visit?"

"Not exactly, but I like to make arrangements ahead of time. It can save us from parking problems and waiting in line. Of course, a good bus driver adds a lot to the trip. I've worked with our driver before, and he's very competent and patient with the kids when they get excited."

"You're a great organizer," Alice said.

"Not at home!" Vera protested. "You know me better than that. If Fred wasn't a compulsive straightener, you wouldn't be able to get in the door. He says my school stuff spreads like crabgrass through every room in the house."

June set their treats in front of them. Vera lifted her Danish whole, while Alice cut the muffin into four neat sections.

"I don't want to lose any of this treat," Vera said, licking icing from her lip with the tip of her tongue. "Don't watch me eat this! I spend too much time in the school cafeteria. Sometimes I think I pick up the kid's bad habits more than I change them."

Alice laughed. "Tell me," she said after a bite of the deli-cious lemony muffin, "have you thought of making a stop at the zoo?"

"I haven't decided what to do in the afternoon," Vera said pensively. "The zoo is something to consider. Kids always love the exotic animals."

"I can't promise anything, but it's possible that Mark could arrange a short tour, something that would fit into your schedule."

"I imagine he would if *you* ask him." Vera grinned, knowing that Alice had a special friendship with Mark Graves, the head veterinarian at the Philadelphia Zoo. He'd been Alice's romantic interest in college, and although they had gone separate ways after their schooling, they were now close friends.

"I'll be happy to." Alice brushed a strand of damp reddish-brown hair from above her warm brown eyes and smiled. "Of course, I can't promise anything until I talk to him."

"I need to firm up the itinerary as soon as possible. The school secretary is going to print it up for me so the kids can take it home on Wednesday."

"I'll talk to him right away if he's available. I don't have to work this weekend. In fact, I'm taking the next ten days off to help with some spring housecleaning at the inn. It's been a long time since I've had a nice block of free time."

"Good for you. You need a break from the hospital. I know teachers desperately need time off in the summer if only to charge up their enthusiasm. Actually, I do a lot of planning for the next year during our off time. Once school starts, it's hard to work on lesson plans and preparations for special projects. I got the idea for a trip to Philadelphia when Fred and I went there last summer."

Alice was so absorbed in her chat with Vera that she hardly noticed when the storm blew itself out and customers started leaving the Coffee Shop.

"Look," Vera said with a chuckle, "we're practically the last people here."

"Shall we walk some more?" suggested Alice

"I'd love to, but Fred is counting on me to watch the store while he runs a couple of errands. Afraid I'd better scurry over there before he thinks we got lost in the tempest."

Alice walked her friend to Fred's Hardware Store, then continued back to the inn. The wind had brought down a number of small branches, but she was relieved to see that there was no major damage around the big Victorian bed-and-breakfast. It would be a job to clean up what had blown onto the spacious yard, so she put it on her mental list of chores for the coming week.

Both her sisters were in the big, comfortable kitchen when she went through the back entrance to avoid dripping rain water in the entry hall.

"Look what the storm blew in," Jane teased, looking pert and younger than her fifty years with a dark ponytail and a casual outfit of jeans and bright-blue knit shirt. "I hope you weren't walking in all that thunder and lightning."

"No, Vera and I holed up at the Coffee Shop. It was fun, but not the long walk we had in mind. I left your gardening boots by the door. Thanks for lending them to me."

"Anytime," Jane said. "How's Vera?"

"She's excited about her class trip. They're going to Philadelphia. I offered to see if Mark can arrange a zoo tour for them."

"Sounds like fun," Louise said, looking up from a pile of receipts that Jane had given her to enter in the inn's account-ing ledger.

Unlike Jane, who preferred to wear jeans and loose-fitting shirts at home, Louise was neatly dressed in a khaki skirt and a light blue blouse that buttoned down the front. Older then Alice by three years, and fifteen years senior to Jane, she was the only one whose hair had turned silver as their father's had in his later years. She was tall, as Daniel Howard had been, with clear blue eyes and fair skin.

"Has Viola phoned yet?" Alice asked.

"Were you expecting a call from her?" Jane finished cutting out a pie crust and turned her attention to the spices she'd set on the counter to flavor her apple filling.

"Not for me, no. Vera and I saw her on our walk before we got chased inside by the storm. She sounded awfully eager to talk to you, Louise."

"I just finished my last lesson for the day. She didn't call while I was with a pupil, did she?" Louise asked Jane.

"No calls at all this morning. That in itself is unusual. Generally when I start baking, the phone rings off the hook."

"Maybe the lightning made Viola hesitate to use the phone," Alice suggested.

"Well, no doubt she'll call when it's convenient for her," Louise said in her usual practical way.

Alice smiled, knowing that Viola had tried more than once to place a kitten with them, but for now they were happy just to have Wendell, the tabby cat who ruled the inn with haughty authority. Viola could never turn away a stray cat, although she tried hard to place new kittens so her home wouldn't be overrun.

"Want a cup of tea, Alice?" Jane asked, ever the hostess, even to her own sisters.

"No thanks. I had tea and a muffin at the Coffee Shop while we were waiting for the storm to subside. I think I'll go upstairs and change. My jeans are damp from splashing through puddles a bit too vigorously, but it was fun except for the lightning."

Just as she got to the doorway, the kitchen phone rang. She went over and picked it up.

"Grace Chapel Inn. This is Alice."

"Alice, has Louise finished her lessons? This is Viola."

"Yes, she's right here." She handed the phone to her sister and hesitated, frankly curious about the weariness she heard in Viola's voice before she left the room.

"Jane is in the process of making a pie," Louise said into the receiver. "Hold on just a moment, Viola, and I'll take your call at the registration desk."

She hurried into the entry hall and picked up the other phone. "Sorry to keep you waiting, Viola," she said. "When Jane is busy with her pots and pans, it can be hard to hear on the kitchen phone."

"Louise, I have a terrible problem." Viola's voice broke, and Louise wondered whether she was crying.

"What's wrong, Viola? Is there something I can help you with?"

"I hate to ask, but you're the only person I would even consider leaving in charge of my store."

Louise was taken aback. She had no idea what to say.

"I'm getting ahead of myself," Viola said with a slight sniff. "My dear Aunt Marion is having heart surgery in Baltimore. She's my father's only sibling, and she helped me so much when he passed on. He died quite young, you know, and I want to be with her now. She never married, and I'm all the family she has."

"Of course you should be there for her," Louise said sympathetically. "If there's anything I can do to help—"

"Oh dear, this is so much to ask, but you're so sensible and competent. What I'm asking is that you be in charge of Nine Lives until I can get back."

"But I don't know a thing about running a bookstore."

"I would just shut it while I'm gone," Viola went on without seeming to hear Louise's misgivings, "but I hate to disappoint my customers, and my classics book club is just getting started. If I close the store and cancel the second meeting, people may lose interest. It's been a dream of mine for years to bring together people who love great books the way I do. Now I have a lovely little group of readers who are eager to meet and discuss great literature. If they see the store is closed and the meeting canceled, they might feel let down."

Louise wondered exactly how much was involved in Viola's request.

"Oh, you won't have to be at the store all the time during the day. I know how busy you are with your lessons and the inn. What I need is a supervisor, someone to keep my helper, Sarah Lister, on track."

"I don't think I've met her."

"She's been working part-time for me, but she's agreed to work full-time while I'm gone. The trouble is, Sarah is a little flighty. I don't mean to be unkind, but she just isn't as steady and reliable as she could be."

"So what you're asking is that I check on your helper from time to time and make sure the store is running smoothly."

"Yes, that's it exactly. And, of course, you would be in charge of the financial aspects, checking out the daily receipts and making bank deposits. I know you keep a firm hand on the accounts for the inn, so my little business should be easy to monitor. I do hope I'm not asking too much of you."

"No, not at all," Louise said graciously. "In fact, it might be fun to play at shopkeeping. At one time I had a secret ambition to run my own music store. Of course, once I married and had my daughter Cynthia, the idea was too impractical. And I'm happy that I came back to Acorn Hill instead."

"The town is fortunate to have you," Viola said with complete sincerity, "and so are your sisters. I know that Alice and Jane don't enjoy the financial details of running the inn, but they contribute in their own special ways. What a wonderful team the three of you are."

"We love working together. But tell me more about what you want me to do."

"I can't tell you how relieved I am. I've been so concerned about how I can leave without letting down my customers and especially the book group. Do you think you could come to the store sometime Monday? I have to leave that afternoon in order to be at the hospital when Aunt Marion has her surgery."

"Yes, that won't be a problem."

"Come any time. Thank you so much, Louise. You don't know how much you've relieved my mind."

"I'm glad to be able to help. I know how worried you must be. Oh, one thing, Viola."

"Yes?"

"The cats?"

"Oh, I've arranged for a neighbor to take care of most of them at my place. My favorite just loves to come to work with me and curl up on the shelf between the gardening books and crafts section. Would you mind terribly?"

Louise breathed a quiet sigh of relief. She could handle one cat. She was fond of cats but glad the care of Viola's many feline friends wouldn't be her responsibility. Her main task would be to make sure Viola's helper could manage on her own during the day. It sounded simple enough, but it was her nature to be a little wary of complications when she was stepping into the unknown.

Chapter  Two

Monday morning Jane cleared away the breakfast dishes left by the inn's two guests, pleased that the elderly couple had especially enjoyed her spoon bread. She'd found a recipe for the baked cornmeal-and-egg dish in her collection of cookbooks.

The inn wasn't fully booked this week, so she had time to catch up on projects and give the kitchen a good cleaning. First, though, she had a new recipe for chicken potpie that she'd been eager to try. Yesterday she'd slow-roasted chicken and cut it into chunks, so she set about enthusiastically making the crust for individual servings.

She rolled the pastry, placed it in small foil pans, diced the potatoes and carrots, and then turned her attention to making her own savory sauce. When she finished, she had eight individual servings lined up on her counter. Three went into the fridge to be baked for dinner, and she began to wrap the remainder to put into the freezer.

As she worked, it occurred to her that an individual pie was the perfect dinner for a person who lived alone, and she felt sure their minister, Rev. Kenneth Thompson, would enjoy one. He was a widower and lived in an apartment above Acorn Hill Antiques. Monday was supposed to be his day off, but he sometimes worked in the church office in the morning. She would take one over to see if she could catch him there.

Jane put one of the pies in a small basket so she wouldn't damage the crust while carrying it, adding a note telling how long to bake it. She went outside, enjoying the brisk morning breeze that had nearly dried the path to the chapel since Saturday's heavy rainfall. She walked carefully, avoiding the few muddy patches where the ground was still soft. A gust of wind blew a small strand of dark hair free of her ponytail, and she brushed it back from her forehead, wishing she hadn't come out without a jacket. Maybe she was so eager for warm spring days that she was rushing the season.

Jane noticed that lights were on in the chapel basement. She went around to the back, passed through the Assembly Room and made her way toward the vesting room, where Kenneth had a desk and church files.

"Good morning," she said softly as she approached it, not wanting to startle him.

"Good morning, Jane. Good to see you."

"I saw lights on and thought you might be down here hard at work."

"No, I just dropped something off. I've been driving around with it since last week, and this was the only place I could think to bring it. Here, take a look at this."

He walked over to a large covered object and removed the blanket that lay over it.

Rev. Thompson was casually dressed in a navy pullover sweater and tan slacks. Even in casual clothes, he had a mildly austere, patrician look. He was tall and lean with short dark hair and hazel eyes. Jane could hear Boston in his accent. The warmth and understanding that he brought to his ministry made even the most critical members of the congregation recognize how fortunate they were to have this fine man as their leader.

"I couldn't resist going to a country auction," he said with a surprisingly boyish grin. "My parents were always taking me along to sales when I was a kid, and the old habit kicked in. Look what I bought."

He didn't need to point it out. Jane's eyes were riveted on the ugliest purple paint she had ever seen. Someone had taken a sturdy, mission-style rocking chair, most likely solid oak, and covered it with a color usually seen only in a child's crayon box.

"My goodness." She didn't know what else to say.

"I'm embarrassed to tell you how little I paid for it," he said with a small smile.

"I guess paint can always be removed," she said, trying to sound optimistic.

"Remove the paint? Whatever for?" He looked confounded.

"Oh, I'm so embarrassed. I just assumed . . . I—"

The minister's laughter kept her from having to continue. "I'm sorry, Jane. I couldn't resist. I certainly agree that the paint must go. But the chair is comfortable. Please try it," he said.

"All right, but no more teasing." She laughed, then sat, holding the little basket with the pie on her lap. "It's really comfortable."

"That's what I thought. And look at the seat."

She stood and looked down at a square of rich, dark leather held in place by vintage brass tacks that appeared to be in almost perfect condition.

"Good that the person who painted it didn't get purple on it," she said. "Unless it was recovered after being painted."

"I doubt that," the pastor said. "The seat is fine quality old leather. That's what attracted me to the chair. Now I have to decide what to do with it."

"You'll want to have it refinished," she suggested. "I love the way the back supports slope down to form the arms. The slatted back and sides look unusually thick and sturdy."

"I did a little research at the library. It's mission oak, probably made around 1900. It could have been made by Stickley Brothers, the most famous makers of oak furniture at that time. I almost hope it wasn't. I didn't pay enough if it is, even with that atrocious paint color."

"Where are you going to have it restored?" Jane asked, her curiosity about the chair fully piqued.

"That's the problem. There's a man in Potterston who does refinishing work, but he uses a dip tank to strip paint. He would have to remove the leather seat, and it's such a good fit I hate to have that done. Also, I'm a great believer in keeping the original patina, if possible. I'm trying to figure out how to do it myself—and where. For now, I thought it would be all right to leave it here for a few days. I don't have a place to work at my apartment."

"That's no problem," Jane said. "You can work in our garden shed. It's not all that large, but there's plenty of ventilation with the door open, and it will be easy to clear a space."

"That's really kind of you, Jane, but I hate to impose on you and your sisters."

"They'll hardly know you're there, and I'm dying of curiosity to see what's under that horrid paint. In fact, I would love to help. There's so much satisfaction in restoring an abused piece of furniture to its original beauty."

"If you're willing to share your time and expertise, I'd be immensely grateful. Even though my parents were in the antiques business, they didn't do any refinishing themselves. They always relied on professionals, but I agree with you about the joy of personally restoring a fine item."

"I'm excited to get at it. Fortunately, we're not fully booked for the next two weeks, unless we get some last-minute reservations. My fingers are itching to start stripping that awful paint. Of course, we should read up a little on techniques before we start, but if I remember right, oak is a marvelous wood to restore. I wonder if it has heavy dark varnish. I'm partial to golden oak myself, but be sure to remind me that it's your chair, not mine."

"I'll bow to your good taste," Rev. Thompson said with a pleased smile.

"You can bring the chair to the shed any time. I'll give you the combination to the lock so you can get in whenever you like. If you have paper and a pencil, I'll write it down."

"On my desk," he said leading the way.

"Oh, by the way, I did have a reason for coming here. I was looking for you."

"Something I can do for you?" he asked.

"No, I made a batch of chicken potpies and, as usual, I went overboard. I was hoping you might like one for your dinner. It has to be baked. I prefer the oven to the microwave."

"Wonderful! Thanks so much, Jane. Thank you for providing an enjoyable break in my day, and thank you for offering your shed and your help. I wish all my problems were so easily solved."

"Is something wrong?"

"Oh, no, not really. Here, you can write the combination on this." His expression had become somber.

She wrote the three numbers on an index card, wondering what was on his mind. His transition from lightheartedness seemed as odd as it was sudden.

He took the combination without looking at it and slid it into the pocket of his trousers.

"Now if you'll excuse me," he said apologetically.

"Of course. I didn't mean to hold you up."

"Oh, you didn't." His denial was automatic, but his mind seemed far away.

"Good-bye then."

She hadn't planned to stay and visit, knowing how busy a minister's schedule could be even on his day off. He could be expecting someone who was coming to him for counseling, or possibly he had an appointment to keep. Even though

Rev. Thompson had been her mentor on a journey of spiritual renewal, she didn't presume on their friendship for special attention. She did hope he would manage to take time for relaxation. He seemed genuinely to appreciate her offer to help with the rocker, and she was glad to be of assistance.

Walking back to the inn, she mulled over her short conversation with the minister. It was at least ten years since he'd suffered the sudden loss of his wife to a heart condition, but Jane knew he still felt the loss very deeply. He was by nature a compassionate man, and his own struggle with sorrow had led him to leave his Boston-area church for a quieter calling in Acorn Hill. Grace Chapel was richly blessed by his ministry. Not only was he a spiritual leader in their congregation, he reached out beyond their church, especially through an ecumenical grief-counseling group at the Potterston Hospital.

Jane had endured the pain of her own unwanted divorce, but the experience made her more sensitive to hidden sorrow. She hoped that he was only distracted by the demands of his job.

Maybe when he came to bring the chair, he would have a few spare minutes. They'd always been able to talk as friends, and she valued that.

When she got back to the inn, Alice was outside picking up fallen twigs and small branches left by Saturday's storm, breaking them up and bagging them as she went.

"Need any help?" Jane offered.

"You can hold the plastic bag if you like. I only have this section of the front left to pick up. That was quite a blow we had, but fortunately we didn't lose any big limbs. Have you been out for a walk?"

"No, I just took a potpie over to the church for Kenneth. He has a rocker to refinish. I told him he can use our shed. I hope you don't mind."

"Of course not. Here, hold the bag while I scoop this pile into it."

Jane absentmindedly complied, thinking about all the miscellaneous jobs that needed to be done around the inn.

"How is Kenneth?" Alice asked.

"Fine, I guess. He was in a bit of a rush."

"Sometimes he reminds me of Father, always taking on the sorrows of the whole congregation. Probably he was concerned about someone's illness or grief."

"Yes, that's probably it," Jane agreed. "Anyway, I gave him the combination to the lock so he can bring his chair to the shed any time. I offered to help him refinish it."

"Of course you did," Alice teased. "There's nothing you like more than a big, messy project."

Jane smiled and gave the bag of lawn debris a big shake to make room for more. "Stripping paint certainly qualifies."

Louise enjoyed the sunshine as she walked toward Nine Lives Bookstore Monday morning. Now that May was only a week away, it finally seemed to be getting warm. The heavy spring rains had left the town looking clean and fresh, and the greens of the trees, bushes and grass seemed especially brilliant.

One of the things she particularly liked about Acorn Hill, the town where she'd grown up, was that almost any place she might want to go was within easy walking distance. Alice and Jane were both enthusiastic walkers, and she'd taken a clue from them and added regular walks to her schedule. The exercise gave her energy, which she needed to keep up with her piano students, church activities and the bookkeeping and other duties at the inn.

She wondered how much time was involved in Viola's request to watch over her store. Louise was glad to help out, but she could squeeze only so much time out of her daily routine. It wouldn't be like her to agree to do a job, then fail to give it the necessary attention.

The Coffee Shop looked busy, judging by the number of cars lining the street in front of it. She walked briskly past, continuing down Chapel Road to Viola's store. Had she more time, she could have stopped in for a pleasant visit with old friends, but her plans today didn't allow time for socializing. Monday was her busy day with students, and she had a full schedule of piano lessons from the time school was out until seven in the evening. Fortunately, Viola closed the store at five every weekday and at noon on Saturday. Somehow Louise would find time to do this favor for her friend.

Nine Lives was housed in a small white building with a red roof, which reminded Louise of an illustration in a children's book. The beveled glass door had the name of the shop and the owner, and Viola had moved a wrought-iron bench outside now that the weather was fair. She kept two large baskets of fresh flowers near the entrance when her garden was in bloom, but today they still held the red and yellow silk bouquets she used in the winter. Inside and out, Viola's pride in her little store made going there a pleasant experience.

Bells rang at the top of the front door when Louise opened it, and immediately she inhaled the pleasing scents of old and new books, freshly brewed coffee and cinnamon-scented potpourri that helped make Nine Lives a mecca for book lovers. Wooden shelves were loaded with books sorted by category and labeled with branded pine signs. The brown carpet and pale taupe walls made the store seem warm and relaxing. Viola had allowed space for portraits of some of her favorite authors, including Dickens, Brontë and Shakespeare. Her English heritage had inspired the ambiance that charmed her customers, the Howard sisters among them.

A cat was curled up on Viola's desk. "Louise, thank you

for coming so early. Sarah will be here at noon, and I hope to be on my way soon after that," Viola said, hurrying to meet her.

"I know you must be eager to get to your aunt," Louise said sympathetically.

Louise believed they were of the same generation, although Viola had never mentioned her age. She was a bit shorter and stouter than Louise and given to wearing long skirts and sturdy sandals at work. Her trademark was a full, colorful scarf that hid a long narrow scar on her neck, a souvenir of an encounter with a fence when she was still a schoolgirl. Today her usually neat cap of soft gray hair seemed electrified, as though the agitation she was feeling had made it bushy. She was wearing a brown skirt with a pale green tunic and a brown and lavender scarf.

"I've left out a big bowl of food for Tess. You won't need to do anything for her. But I'd better tell you about Sarah. She's a lovely girl but . . . not exactly suited to working in a bookstore."

"She does know how to handle the daily routine, doesn't she?" Louise asked, trying not to sound worried.

"Oh yes, I trust her to mind the store while I'm gone—with a little supervision from you when you have a chance. The truth is, she's the niece of a friend of mine. Her aunt lives in Potterston and is one of the members of my new book club. You'll love Hannah. Her mother was a war bride from England after World War II. We met at a book fair in Philadelphia and became fast friends after we discovered a mutual love of classical books and all things British."

Louise wasn't sure how this related to her promise to help out at the store, but she waited patiently to find out exactly what it was that Viola expected of her.

"Anyway," Viola continued after taking a breath, "my friend Hannah agreed that Sarah could live with her while she decides what to do with her life. She started college, then dropped out to try becoming a fashion model. Unfortunately that didn't work out, and her parents are a bit cross with her. Hannah is a widow and doesn't have children, so she thought it would be delightful to have her brother's daughter living with her for a while. Sarah is a lovely girl, pleasant and polite. I'm sure you'll take to her."

"I'm sure she's very nice," Louise said, wondering where all this was leading.

"The thing is," Viola said with a deep sigh, "she tends to be a bit awkward when she does things. She tries hard to be helpful, but things always seem to get a tad muddled when she puts her hand to them. For instance, I told her to shelve some new books in the mystery section one afternoon while I went to a dental appointment. When I got back, they were all in the gardening and health and history sections. Sarah thought mystery lovers would like to do a little detective work to find the latest titles. She left little clues on sticky notes."

"Oh, my," Louise said, not knowing what else to say.

"I tried to explain that book buyers don't have time to play games to find what they want. When she tried to retrieve the new titles and put them where they belong, she couldn't decipher her own clues. Not that she isn't an intelligent girl." Viola, who was not given to saying unkind things about others, struggled for the right description. "She just gets carried away sometimes. She doesn't think things through. That's why I can't totally rely on her to run the store. Not that you have to be here all day supervising. Just make sure she doesn't make any radical changes on her own initiative."

"I think I understand," Louise said, although Viola's assessment of the girl gave her pause. "She'll be here every day?"

"Yes, you can rely on that. I originally hired her to work part-time, but she's happy to work full-time while I'm gone. She'll open the store in the mornings. I've already given her the spare key. She knows the routine to close also, but I told her you would take care of the receipts and the banking. Let me explain how I operate."

Louise followed her friend to the back room where things weren't nearly as tidy and organized as they were in the front of the store.

"Since I've been selling antique books on the Internet, I've begun to run out of space," Viola said, apologizing for the books that covered shelves, a table, several chairs and her desk, spilling over into stacks on the floor. "I haven't advertised any books since I found out about my aunt's surgery, so there's nothing you need to do with that part of the business. Sarah knows to check my e-mail every day and tell potential customers that I'll get to them as soon as I return from a family emergency."

Viola explained her accounting system, and Louise's responsibilities seemed fairly simple. She would make daily deposits at the bank and keep the shop supplied with low-denomination bills and change for the register. Viola had taken care of paying all outstanding bills and only needed Louise to make entries into her daily account book. All told, Louise thought her duties would take less than half an hour a day—not much time at all to help a friend.

"What I really hate to miss is the next session of my classics book club," Viola said. "We're just getting started, and the members are so enthusiastic. I've written everything down, along with a list of those who were at the first meeting. I'm providing refreshments for the next meeting. I'll have to leave arranging that up to you and Sarah, I'm afraid. There's cash in my safe to cover it. I've written down the combination. Now, have I told you everything?"

"I think so," Louise said, trying to sort out her responsibilities.

"I can't forget the most important thing of all: our selection for the meeting. The group decided to begin with *A Christmas Carol* by Charles Dickens. Oh, I know, it's not the right season for a Christmas story, but the group wants to begin by reading and discussing Dickens. They decided to start with the best known of his works, and it's short enough that everyone was sure it could be read in time to discuss it at the next meeting. He got paid by the word, you know, and because he was always in need of money, he wrote some very long novels, but this isn't one of them. I laid aside a copy for you. Here it is."

Louise took the book, a thick red volume with gold lettering on the spine.

"Don't worry. It's a collection of his stories. You'll only need to read *A Christmas Carol*. It ends on page seventy-four."

"I need to read it?" Louise was puzzled.

"Didn't I mention? I was supposed to lead the discussion, but I'm sure you won't have any trouble filling in. They're a wonderful group, so full of ideas and eager to talk about what they've read. Just prepare a few simple questions, and the members will take it from there."

"Dickens really isn't my specialty," Louise demurred.

"You'll love reading the original. So many of the film versions have been pretty dreadful, in my opinion. There's no substitute for a good novel. Now, is there anything I haven't told you? Let me think." She paused, lost in thought for a moment. "No, that should cover it. Sarah is a sweet girl. She always means well. I'm sure she'll do a splendid job for you. She's coming at noon today, and then I'll be off. I won't be easy in my mind until I know my aunt's surgery is successful. I'll leave her number, and I'll keep in touch in case you have any questions."

"Yes, please do," Louise said, her mind still reeling at the prospect of monitoring a flighty employee and leading a book group. She could only trust that her obligations seemed more complicated than they really were.

"And so, as Tiny Tim proclaimed, 'God bless us, every one!'" Viola smiled, some of the worry lines on her face softening.

"I'll pray for your aunt's return to health," Louise said. "I hope she makes a quick recovery."

She trusted that it wasn't selfish to want Viola to come home soon. With a guilty start, she found Scrooge's famous words going through her head, "Bah! Humbug!"

As she walked back to the inn, she reminded herself that God never gave her a heavier burden than she was able to bear. No doubt this new responsibility would be a learning experience. By the time she got home, she was looking forward to reading Dickens's famous story. Life was so much harder in Victorian times that his tale would serve to make her even more grateful for the blessings in her own life.

Chapter  Three

The inn's two elderly guests enjoyed Tuesday's breakfast and lingered over the meal longer than usual. Jane served a creamy egg casserole. The meal began with freshly squeezed orange juice and included a basket of warm rolls and cranberry muffins. The couple remained at the table, enjoying multiple cups of hazelnut coffee, so it was almost midmorning before Jane could clear the table and clean up the kitchen.

While she worked, her thoughts kept straying to their minister. She'd seen him in many situations, some very stressful, but he'd seemed different yesterday, a bit more pensive than usual.

Or maybe she was imagining things. It was his day off, and perhaps he'd been eager to do the kinds of errands that have to be done on a free day.

She gathered the drip pans from under the stove burners, intent on scrubbing them clean, but another idea came to her. Had he brought his purple chair to the shed? He could easily have come and gone without her noticing. Just to satisfy her curiosity, she abandoned her task and went out to the shed.

It was locked to protect neighborhood children who might be tempted to investigate the interior and hurt themselves on the tools and gardening equipment. Jane had the door open in a jiffy and stepped into the murky interior. Even without turning on the light, she could see that items had been rearranged so that the chair could be positioned on a drop cloth in the middle of the floor.

What possible decorating scheme called for a chair that color? She had chosen a reddish-purple shade called Oriental Eggplant for her own bedroom, but the color on the chair was a dreadful one, heavy with gunmetal gray and devoid of any redeeming characteristics. In fact, it looked like the person who painted it had used up some odds and ends of paint by mixing them together. Still, she could visualize how the sturdy, well-made chair would look when it was restored to its original finish. Rev. Thompson was certainly right about the leather seat. Burnished by years of use, it had rich nut-brown coloring but none of the cracking or worn spots typical of aging leather.

She was eager to start stripping off the offensive paint, but she had to remember it was her friend's project, not hers. He would let her know when he was ready to begin.

Back in the kitchen, she thought again of her minister's mood. That was one thing about her profession: A chef had a lot of time to think while managing the kitchen and preparing food. Her own life was a tranquil one, so maybe she was looking too hard for drama in other people's lives.

When her kitchen chores were done, she remembered her promise to provide refreshments for a guild meeting the next evening. Even though she preferred making things from scratch, she did have a nice recipe for German-chocolate layer bars using a cake mix. She had the sour cream and sweetened condensed milk on hand, and she always kept a supply of chopped nuts in the freezer. If she frosted them using her special milk chocolate recipe, the bars would be as delicious as any she might make from scratch.

What made this recipe special was the shredded coconut she spread over the bars. When they were cooled and frosted, she cut them into convenient squares and put them in a covered carrier. They would stay fresh for days, so there was no reason not to carry them over to the church now and leave them in the kitchen.

Rev. Thompson's SUV was in its usual parking place, and Jane elected to go into the church through the front door. `

She loved the interior of the chapel, especially the stained-glass windows that told visual stories from the life of Christ. Her favorite was Jesus holding a lamb, but she always thought of her father when she looked at the scene of the Ascension, his favorite window. She stood in contemplation for several moments before noticing that she wasn't alone. The chapel's minister was kneeling before the altar.

Jane hurried down to the lower level as quietly as possible. The last thing she wanted to do was interrupt a person at prayer. She left her bars in the kitchen and silently departed by the back exit, taking care to ease the door shut without making any noise.

On the way home, she told herself that it was a natural thing for a minister of God to seek spiritual guidance in His sanctuary. No doubt the pastor prayed regularly at the altar. Seeing him there didn't signify that he had some special problem. Even if he did, she was a friend and a member of the congregation. If he wanted to share something with her, she would listen gladly. Otherwise, she owed him the gift of privacy.

Even in a town as special as Acorn Hill, news and rumors spread rapidly. Aunt Ethel, who lived in the inn's carriage house, was proof of that. Although she'd been a farm wife before her husband's death, she took to life in the town with gusto. She made it her business to know everything that was happening, and she delighted in being a news source for her nieces.

Jane resolved not to say another word about Rev. Thompson, not even to her sisters, although she trusted their discretion completely. For her own part, she would remember him in her prayers and hope that he wasn't facing a crisis of some kind. Sometimes being a good friend meant stepping back and waiting to be asked for help.

Alice spent most of the morning washing windows inside. Both of her sisters considered it the worst of chores, but she rather liked putting a shine on glass. She kept at it diligently, but by early afternoon her shoulders and arms were beginning to protest. If there was one thing the inn had in abundance, it was glass. She went from windows to mirrors before she finally gave up for the day. By consent, they hired a local handyman to do the outside of the windows and to clean the rain gutters rather than risk climbing on ladders themselves.

Jane had left the filling for shrimp-salad sandwiches in the fridge because they'd agreed at breakfast that their schedules were too full for lunch together at a set time. Alice was the last to take a lunch break, and she was tired enough to enjoy a quiet interlude in her day. She toasted two pieces of Jane's homemade caraway-rye bread and spread the shrimp, celery and green-grapes mixed with Jane's special mayo over the toast.

What a blessing it was to have Jane fixing all their meals even when they didn't have time to eat together, Alice thought as she silently said grace before beginning her lunch. Sometimes she liked to read when she ate alone, but today she was content to let her mind wander and her muscles relax. There was something healing about quiet moments alone.

When the phone rang, she was reluctant to answer it, even though she wasn't on call at the hospital this week. Still, it might be a potential guest, so she couldn't ignore it.

"Alice, I'm glad I found you at home," Vera said, not needing to identify herself.

"Aren't you at school?" Alice asked, surprised to hear from her friend so early in the afternoon.

"Yes, but I have an urgent favor to ask of you."

"Is everyone all right?"

"Yes," Vera assured her with a faint laugh. "It's not that kind of an emergency. I just have to ask you something. You're my last hope. I hate to impose on your good nature, but do you think you could chaperone on my class trip?"

"Go along to Philadelphia on the bus?" Alice asked to give herself time to consider Vera's request.

"It's next Monday, the last day of April. I told you that I had enough chaperones, but one of them has canceled. Worse, she was scheduled to be in charge of a group of boys. The principal supervised my class while I called every one of my parents whom I thought might be willing. I even asked Fred, and he would be willing, but he has a doctor's appointment in Potterston, one he really shouldn't miss because he's been having trouble with arthritis in his shoulder." Vera wound down, seemingly out of breath.

"I don't know whether I would be very good at it."

Alice's first instinct had been to agree immediately, but she wasn't at all sure she was qualified to be in charge of boys on a field trip. She loved working with the girls in her ANGELs group at church, but they were older than the children in Vera's class. They liked to talk about boys, but what Alice had learned secondhand about teenage males would be no help at all in keeping track of fifth graders.

"I won't blame you if you say no," Vera said somewhat dejectedly, "but I have every confidence that you would do an outstanding job. They'll be excited, and sometimes they get a little rowdy, but they're all nice boys, really. My problem is that so many parents work and can't get time off to chaperone a trip, but the school rules are very specific. If

I don't find one more adult to go, the trip to Philadelphia will have to be canceled."

"I suppose the children would be terribly disappointed," Alice said hesitantly.

"Devastated! They've been looking forward to it for a long time."

"I guess there's no reason why I can't go." Alice tried to sound enthusiastic but didn't quite manage it.

"I know what a huge favor this is," Vera said, relief in every word. "I wouldn't ask if I could think of anyone else. No, that doesn't sound right. You would be my first choice, but I hate to impose on our friendship."

"You're not imposing," Alice said. "I'm happy to help. I just hope I'm up to the job."

Long after Vera ended their conversation to hurry back to her class, Alice kept hoping that she would be an adequate chaperone. There was no way she could say no to a close friend like Vera, and it would be an awful shame if the class outing had to be canceled. Still, a nagging doubt lingered. What if she lost track of one of the children in her group? What if one of them got hurt or caused damage? Maybe the boys wouldn't obey her. After all, she was neither a teacher nor a parent. How would she handle it if they ignored her or, even worse, misbehaved?

Vera made it sound easy, but she had years of experience teaching children. She had a natural gift for working with them. Alice did see school-age children at the hospital, but supervising them was entirely different when they were injured or ill. She knew what to do then.

She'd given her word. She would go, but the prospect made cleaning windows seem easy.

∞

Jane put a second coating of glaze on her stuffed pork chops and returned them to the oven to keep them warm. Ethel was always pleased when Jane served this recipe, because it was basically hers. Jane used the crumbled cornbread, onions and chopped green peppers called for in the original list of ingredients but added her own touches, especially in the glaze. Ketchup and brown sugar alone were too sweet for her taste, so she added mustard and chili powder. As many times as she'd served the modified dish, her aunt had never seemed to notice the difference.

As much as she liked a good meal, Ethel took more pleasure in the company of her nieces than in the food, and they were all glad that she lived nearby. She was their father's half sister, perhaps in her midseventies, although she was secretive about her exact age. When her husband, Bob Buckley, passed on and her children moved away, she was terribly lonely on their farm. Her move to Acorn Hill and the carriage house had been a happy alternative. A bit plump with pale blue eyes and tinted bright-red hair cut short, she loved to talk and made it her mission to socialize with as many townsfolk as possible. She took pride in knowing what was happening. Jane reminded herself not to mention anything about the chapel or its minister that might provide fuel for gossip. Ethel wouldn't intentionally break a confidence, but she would suffer if she couldn't share everything she knew.

Jane heard footsteps in the front hall and knew her aunt had arrived. Ethel came into the kitchen wearing an emerald green and brilliant blue dress in a cheerful floral pattern.

"Aunt Ethel, you're looking pretty this evening," Jane said as she put a bowl of tossed salad on the table.

"My Bob used to like a dress similar to this one. Of course, there wasn't much opportunity to wear it when we lived on the farm."

Talking to her aunt didn't keep Jane from tossing French-cut sweet potato fries that had browned in the oven.

"Something smells delicious," Ethel said, trying to get a glimpse.

"Now you know you like to be surprised," Jane teased. "Anyway, Alice and Louise will be down in a minute. Dinner is nearly ready."

Her sisters were prompt, arriving on the dot of six. They knew that timing was important to Jane, who disliked letting food overcook. Louise asked their aunt to give the blessing.

Both her sisters seemed distracted this evening, and Jane found herself talking to Ethel most of the time. Of course, her aunt never lacked for conversation, so she was easy to entertain.

"I heard that Viola Reed's aunt is bad," she said.

Louise looked up with a start, as though she'd just joined them.

"Yes, she's having surgery in Baltimore. I'm helping with the store while she's gone."

"My, how can you possibly do that with all your lessons?" Ethel asked.

"I won't have to be there to run the store, just to supervise and handle the receipts. The only part that concerns me is her book group. She wants me to lead the literary discussion. I have to confess that I don't feel qualified."

"What are they reading?" Jane asked.

"Dickens's *A Christmas Carol*."

"But it's nowhere near Christmas," their aunt was quick to point out.

"Yes, but it's the shortest of his well-known works, and the group wanted to start with something everyone could finish by the next meeting."

"I always found that story a bit creepy," Ethel said. "Scrooge was so mean, and the ghosts still scare me."

"I guess that's part of the book's appeal. Many people like to be a little scared. I imagine we'll be discussing the author's style and the Victorian setting and such," Louise said without much conviction. "I've never been to a book club, so this is all new."

"You'll do fine," Ethel said. "You always do."

"You're not the only one facing a challenge," Alice said, breaking a long silence. "Vera asked me to chaperone her class trip to Philadelphia next Monday. I'll be in charge of a group of boys."

"You'll be great at that," Jane assured her, noticing that neither of her sisters was eating much. "Look at how successful your ANGELs have been at church."

"There's a big difference between dealing with middleschool girls and fifth-grade boys," Alice said with a wan smile. "I don't know a thing about boys that young. I suspect I'll have my hands full."

By the time Jane served baked pears with soft custard for dessert, the talk had turned to town gossip. Jane was feeling decidedly sleepy by the time the meal concluded and her aunt left for home. Louise and Alice helped her clean up. Then both pleaded fatigue and went up to their own rooms. Jane found that all she really wanted to do was go to bed early, but she still had preparations for the next day's breakfast.

∽

The school bus was full, every seat occupied by children, but something dreadful seemed to have happened. Alice hurried down the aisle, looking frantically on either side. She saw a girl with pale yellow braids. Beside her, a small, dark-eyed girl was saying something Alice couldn't understand. The seat at the back that went all the way across the bus had several girls squeezed together.

Alice started back toward the front, more frantic now, looking intently at every little girl she passed. What was Jane doing on this bus, a very young Jane with her dark ponytail held by a big yellow flower? Alice wanted to talk to her, but she had to find the boys.

Where were the boys? She'd promised to keep them safe,

and now she couldn't find them, not even one. Had they run away or been taken away? Maybe they'd been left at the school. She wanted to ask Vera, but her friend was too busy talking to the bus driver to pay any attention. Mr. Preston, an elderly friend of Alice's father, was driving the bus. How could that be? The kindly old man had been ancient when Alice was young.

Terrified now, Alice ran to the back of the bus again. She wanted to call out the names of the missing boys, but she couldn't remember any of them.

"Stop the bus! Stop the bus!" she called instead, but old Mr. Preston didn't seem to hear her.

"You have to watch the boys yourself," Vera said, finally speaking to her. "Where have you lost them?"

"I didn't lose them," Alice whispered fearfully. "They just disappeared."

"Boys can't disappear," Vera said in a stern voice, sounding just like Mrs. Graham, the teacher who had frightened Alice in kindergarten when she was too shy to participate in show-and-tell. "It's all your fault, Alice Howard. You should have tied them together."

"I don't know what to do with boys," Alice cried.

"Don't be a baby," the Mrs. Graham voice chided. "Put the boys in a sack, then you'll know where they are."

"They won't be able to breathe," the nurse in Alice said. "Boys have to be able to breathe."

"Bah! Humbug!" old Mr. Preston said. "I can't have noisy boys on my bus."

"But they were on your bus," Alice insisted. "What did you do with them?"

"They were your responsibility," the bus driver said. "Everyone knows boys need to be watched."

"Let me off! Let me off! I'll go back and look."

"It's too late, Alice." Vera had Mrs. Graham's face now.

"You lost the boys. Do you know what happens to chaperones who lose boys? Do you know? Do you know?"

"I didn't mean to. Didn't mean to—"

Alice sat upright in bed, panic bringing her to
wakefulness.

"I lost the boys," she said, slow to make the transition
from dream to reality. "But I would never do that. I know
they must be watched."

She shook her head, willing the nightmare to go away.
She was back in her own room, the phantom bus receding
from her mind, but the fear was slow to disappear.

"I would never lose a child," she said out loud, trying to
convince herself that the fear was as unreal as the bad dream.
"Lord, help me. I never want to fail a child."

Slowly the room around her materialized. The luminous
dial on her alarm clock showed that it was only a few minutes after three, the depth of the night. She swung her toes
over the edge of the bed and stood, shaken by the way her
frightening dream had mirrored her real fears.

Usually she slept soundly through the night. If she had
nightmares, they were ordinarily forgotten as soon as she
opened her eyes in the morning. She believed, quite sensibly,
that dreams were only a way of working through the impres-
sions that lingered from the waking hours. Every healthy person dreamed. It was housecleaning for the brain. She told
herself all this as she tried to put the bad dream behind her.

The details didn't fade as they should have. She still felt
the loss of the boys she'd meant to protect, although she
didn't have the foggiest idea why she'd lost them.

She turned on her bedside light, but the soft glow didn't
bring any comfort. Nor did the prospect of returning to her
bed appeal to her. As quietly as she could, she slipped into
her flowery housecoat, pushed her feet into fuzzy slippers
and opened the door of her bedroom. She shared the third

floor with Louise and Jane, and both their doors were shut.
Not wanting to wake them, she quietly went down two flights
of stairs to the main floor.

Her first impulse was to make a cup of tea, but instead
she went into the library, where she had spent many happy
hours with her father, often in companionable silence as he
worked at his desk or read.

Without turning on a light, she found his chair and
curled up in it with one of the tapestry throw pillows
clutched against her. She thought back to the bad dreams of
childhood, although the details had long since faded. What
she could recall was the loving assurance her father had given
her when she was frightened in the night. He'd always been
able to calm her fears and make the bad images go away.

She closed her eyes and let his love return to her.

∞

Usually the first one up, Jane was surprised to find the door
to the library open. She peeked in and was even more surprised to see Alice curled up in a chair sound asleep.

She looked with tenderness at her sister and silently
asked the Lord's blessing on her. Smiling to herself, she
quietly closed the door.

Chapter  Four

Jane went to the shed as soon as breakfast was over Wednesday morning. The purple rocker was undisturbed in the center of the floor, and she wondered when Rev. Thompson wanted to begin removing the old finish. She would gladly do it for him, but she sensed that he wanted to be involved in the project. Otherwise, he probably would have found a professional who would provide expert restoration.

Spring cleaning was a family tradition with the Howards, but her sisters urged her to confine her activities to the kitchen and garden. They believed that she did more than her share in running the inn, although Jane loved her work so much that it never seemed like toil to her.

Still, she appreciated the time to work in the garden. She wanted to think about a water feature, possibly a little fountain, but only if it was a project she could handle herself. Replanting and expanding the garden gave her time to think about his long devotion to the Lord's service and her own renewed faith. Coming back to Acorn Hill to run the bed-and-breakfast with her sisters had led her to believe that the Lord had a plan for her. She only needed to listen to the still voice within and be willing to follow where He led.

"I'm leaving now, Jane," Louise called out from the front of the garden. "I'll be at the bookstore."

Jane walked toward her sister, pulling off her cotton gardening gloves. "Will you be back for lunch?"

"Don't wait for me. I don't know how much time I'll need to spend at the store. I'll be meeting Viola's helper for the first time."

"Well, good luck," Jane said cheerfully, knowing that Louise could handle any challenge.

"I hope no one wants to change a lesson time, but if you do get any calls, say I'll get back to them this evening."

"No problem," Jane agreed, admiring her sister as she walked away.

Louise had been in her teens when their mother died, and she had willingly taken over many of the responsibilities of raising Jane. Thanks to Louise, and to Alice too, Jane's childhood had been happy in spite of the loss of her mother. Both her sisters had fond memories of Madeleine Howard, but Jane had none at all. Still, she always felt that she had been doubly blessed in her sisters.

She pulled her straw hat farther down on her forehead so it wouldn't blow off, then resumed energetically reshaping a particularly wild bush.

∞

There was only one customer in the bookstore when Louise got there, an unusually short woman in her midfifties who was active in the Methodist Church. Louise knew her by sight but not by name.

"Good morning," Louise said, looking around for someone who matched Viola's description of her helper.

She checked the back of the store and noted that Tess was curled up on the desk and her food dish was nearly full, but the small restroom was not in use. As far as she could determine, Sarah Lister was nowhere in the store. She checked the front again, but there really were few places in the tidy little shop that could conceal someone.

"I've been waiting at least ten minutes for help," the customer said to Louise. She shrugged and sighed with frustration. "Viola knows I can't reach the shelf where she keeps the home-and-garden books. I was really hoping to find something on building a patio before my husband and I contract with someone to put one in for us. It helps so much to have a picture to show."

"Viola's aunt is having surgery, so she went to Baltimore to see her through it. Her helper should be here, but I'll be glad to reach any books you would like to see."

Louise spent the next few minutes taking down and returning books to the shelf until the woman decided which one to buy. Louise was patient with the customer but increasingly mystified regarding Sarah Lister's whereabouts. People were honest in Acorn Hill, yet it was still better not to leave a retail establishment untended. There was no knowing how many sales might be missed because no clerk was on the premises.

By the time she completed her first sale, Louise noted the arrival of another customer. A mother with two toddlers came to look for a birthday gift for an older child. Louise didn't know what to recommend, but she did her best to entertain the little ones while the customer leisurely browsed the selections. Fortunately, Viola kept a few books and puzzles for children at a little corner table, and Louise spent what seemed like a long time reading storybooks to a wide-eyed little blonde girl and her rambunctious brother. By the time the mother left with the book she'd purchased, twenty minutes or more had passed since Louise's arrival, and there was no sign of the missing assistant.

"This is not good," Louise said under her breath just as the bell over the front door sounded again.

The girl who entered was tall and rail thin with short, dark brown hair falling over one eye and tucked behind her ear on the other side. She was wearing a lacy white tunic and a short lavender skirt that revealed long, pale legs with feet thrust into platform shoes that added several more inches to her impressive height. She matched Viola's description of Sarah, and Louise wasn't sure how to handle her absence from the store.

"Is there something I can help you with?" the young woman asked, looking at Louise with hazel eyes that seemed to dance with gold and green flecks.

"I'm not a customer," Louise said, remembering that a calm demeanor was most often helpful in working with her piano students. "I'm Louise Howard, Viola's friend. I came to see what I could do to help with the store. You are Sarah Lister, aren't you?"

"Yes, I went over to the Coffee Shop for a few minutes. Customers like a lot of time to browse," she said cheerfully.

"I made two sales while you were gone."

Louise didn't want to scold, but Viola had given her the responsibility of making sure everything was all right. An absentee clerk was unacceptable.

"Oh, I didn't realize. I'm so sorry. I was talking to this really cute guy who's working as a landscaper this summer. He's really friendly, and time just got away from me. I'm really sorry. I want to do a good job for Ms. Reed."

"She has a lot of confidence in you," Louise assured her, trying to be as positive as possible.

"She's been a real sweetheart, letting me work here while I decide what to do next. I wanted to be a model, but it's not easy to get started. My folks didn't want me just hanging out, hoping to get discovered, so I desperately needed some kind of job."

She seemed to say all that in one breath, fiddling with the hair behind her ear while she talked.

"It won't happen again. I promise," she said, sounding genuinely contrite.

"I can relieve you for a lunch break, if you like," Louise offered, "but you really shouldn't leave the store untended."

"No, never again," she said solemnly. "Anyway, I gave him my phone number at my aunt's in Potterston, and my cell phone number. If he wants to talk any more, he knows where to reach me."

"Maybe we can go over your duties in the store," Louise said, changing the subject. "I've never worked in a bookstore, so there are things you can teach me."

"I'll be glad to tell you anything I can. Of course, I haven't been working here very long. Ms. Reed knew I didn't have any experience, but she and my aunt are good friends. They just love to go on and on about books."

Some part of Sarah was always in motion. She fiddled with her hair, shifted from foot to foot in the uncomfortable-looking platforms, or wrung her hands.

"I thought perhaps you were reading *A Christmas Carol* to help with the discussion group," Louise said.

Sarah gave her a blank look.

"You know, the book by Charles Dickens. I understood you're going to help with the meeting."

"Oh, that. I've seen the movie twice," Sarah said dismissively. "All I have to do for the book club is open the store for the evening and arrange for refreshments and serve them. Why do you suppose they're reading about Christmas in April?"

Louise didn't try to explain, but she suspected that Sarah wasn't any more interested in an explanation than she was in reading the book.

Louise thought it would be a good idea to stay at the store for a while. Viola trusted Sarah, but the girl had never had to do her job without supervision. Before Louise could say anything else, the door opened again and an elderly man entered.

"Good morning, Mr. Trotty," Sarah called out cheerfully. "How is your bike running today?"

He grunted something that Louise didn't quite catch and

walked over to the section of outdoor books, immediately picking up a thick volume on freshwater fishing.

Mr. Trotty on his bike was a familiar sight in Acorn Hill. He made regular rounds of the park and the rest of the town in almost any weather. A widower who lived alone, he rarely spoke to anyone. The common belief was that he was hard of hearing, but the truth was that he could hear well enough. He just let his mind wander on occasion, and drivers who knew him were especially cautious when they saw him on the road. He was known to dart across traffic without looking in either direction.

Sarah walked to the back room, leaving him to his own devices.

"I promised to unpack some books Ms. Reed bought at an auction," she said.

Louise followed, quietly suggesting that Sarah attend to the customer first.

"Oh, he never buys anything. He only looks at pictures in the fishing book for a few minutes, then leaves. Ms. Reed said it's perfectly all right. She offered to give him the book once, but he didn't want it to take it home." She smiled and her eyes showed compassion. "I think he likes to have a place to go every day."

"Yes, I suspect you're right," Louise said, appreciative of Sarah's perceptiveness. "Is there something I can do to help you, Sarah?"

"Oh, I don't know." She looked perplexed. "The shelves always need straightening and dusting, but that's my job, really. It helps pass the time. Some days here seem so long. I don't think the book business is for me—not that I'm not grateful to Ms. Reed for giving me something to do while I think about my career."

Louise cleared a small space on the desk and sat down to enter yesterday's receipts into the book. She hadn't planned on staying long, but she wasn't comfortable about leaving the girl alone in the store. Still, Viola had confidence in Sarah, and employing her was Viola's decision. Louise had just made up her mind to leave when Sarah gasped and jumped away from a shelf of falling books.

Books rained all over the already crowded floor. The top shelf was still intact, but somehow Sarah had started an avalanche of hardcover volumes that now lay in disarray, some open or partially open with their spines and pages in jeopardy.

"I guess it was too full," she said weakly, rubbing her arm where one had scraped it. "Sorry. I guess I should have stood on something. I can usually reach everything without any trouble. You must think I'm a terrible klutz."

"No, you're just having a bad day," Louise said kindly, hoping she was right.

Before they could begin picking up books, the bell over the door sounded and a woman entered. As soon as she was in the store, Mr. Trotty carefully replaced the fishing book and scurried away.

When Louise saw who the newcomer was, she wished she could make a quick exit too. Florence Simpson was standing by the register, tapping her fingers on the counter.

Louise knew her well. Florence was a stout woman in her late sixties with finely penciled eyebrows and gray eyes. Today she was dressed in a pink-and-orange floral-print dress and beige high heels. She topped off her outfit with a stiff-brimmed yellow straw hat festooned with flowers, and she carried a large beige leather purse.

Louise and Florence had worked together on several church projects, and Louise usually found such ventures exhausting. Florence was well intentioned, but she tended to be very strong-minded, sometimes to the point of being combative.

Sarah went over to her and politely asked if she could help her.

"I need to speak to Viola," Florence said emphatically.

"I'm sorry, but she's not here."

"When will she be back?"

"She wasn't sure. Her aunt is having surgery in Baltimore."

"Do you mean that she left you in charge of Nine Lives?" There was no mistaking the displeasure in Florence's voice.

"Yes. I mean, not entirely."

Sarah seemed to shrink away, and Louise felt that she had no choice but to intervene. Florence could be somewhat overbearing when unopposed.

"Hi, Florence. I'm helping out too," she said, stepping into the store where Florence could see her.

"Louise, I didn't know you were here."

"What can we do for you?" Louise deliberately included Sarah in the discussion by standing beside her. "I'm only here as an adviser. Sarah is quite capable of seeing to your needs."

"I ordered a book ages ago, and I still haven't gotten it," Florence complained. "I'm sure if Viola were here, she would be most upset."

"I'm sorry, Mrs. Simpson," Sarah said. "Your book is on back order with her suppliers. We'll let you know the minute it comes in."

"Shouldn't you check your computer or something?" Florence asked suspiciously.

"No, Mrs. Simpson. Ms. Reed specifically mentioned your order before she left. She's checked all possible sources. The book has been out of print for ages, but she'll get it for you if anyone can."

"I want a nice fresh copy, not some shabby beat-up one."

"I understand," Sarah said.

"Viola has always been able to get the books I want. Maybe she's been too upset by her aunt's poor health."

"Ms. Reed has done everything that can possibly be done regarding your request. You know, not many people are reading Clara Louise Burnham these days."

"Which is a terrible shame," Florence said. "She was a cheerful, inspiring author and possibly a distant relative of my grandaunt. She wrote this wonderful book about a widower who made the mistake of marrying a young girl who only wanted his money. It takes a little hunchbacked woman to straighten everything out."

"You sound like you already know the story," Louise said.

"I know of it," Florence said a bit indignantly. "I wouldn't be so eager to get a copy if I'd read it. It was only by chance that I came across a postcard advertisement. It was tucked into one of the books my mother left me."

"I'll let you know the minute we get a lead on it," Sarah promised.

"Very well. If I don't hear from you, I'll check in again in a week or so. If you talk to Viola, tell her that I hope her aunt is doing well. Nice seeing you, Louise."

Florence hurried toward the door, a bit unsteady on heels not well designed for walking. Louise had observed before that no matter how long she lingered to talk, Florence always liked to give the impression that she was late for a very important appointment.

"You handled that very nicely," Louise said, happy to be able to compliment Sarah.

The girl did have a good attitude. She was courteous and helpful with customers. If she kept her mind on what she was doing, everything would be all right. At least Louise hoped so.

∞

"Jane," a familiar voice called out from the front entrance, unlocked during the day so the inn's guests could come and go as they liked.

Jane hurried out from the kitchen, taking care not to trip over Wendell, their gray tabby, who had been haunting the kitchen hoping for a treat. She was happy to see that

Rev. Thompson was her visitor. He was dressed in a charcoal suit and highly polished black shoes; obviously he hadn't come to work on the chair.

"I'm glad you're here," he said. "I want to be sure the rocking chair isn't in your way."

"No, not at all. Come back to the kitchen and have a cup of tea."

"All right, but I can only stay a few minutes."

Jane already had the kettle heating, so she had steaming cups of orange spice tea on the table in moments. She put out a plate of freshly baked vanilla cookies and sat down across from the minister.

"I just wanted you to know that I won't be able to work on the chair as soon as I thought," he said, running his fingers over the cup handle.

"Any time is fine."

Jane wondered whether that was his real reason for coming. He seemed unusually distracted, making only a halfhearted attempt at small talk.

"I appreciate it. Some day soon I'll go to Fred's Hardware and see what paint stripper he recommends."

"You can rely on his judgment," Jane agreed.

There was a long silence between them, and she felt that there was something else he wanted to say.

"I know how busy a minister can be," she said to fill the silence. "Father was always on the run, especially when a member of the congregation was in the hospital or facing a crisis."

"I'll be gone overnight," he said in a somber tone.

"I hope there's not a problem with the congregation." She said the only thing that occurred to her.

"No, it's personal."

She sipped her tea, waiting to hear more, but he seemed lost in thought as his drink cooled in front of him.

"The truth is," he said slowly, "I have an interview."

"Oh?"

"A job interview. I'm being considered for a position in the church's radio ministry."

She was stunned. "That would mean leaving Grace Chapel!"

"I'm afraid so. I don't know for certain that I'll be offered the position, but this will be my second interview. I've always had an interest in radio. I learned about broadcasting in high school and hosted a local show after I graduated."

"I don't know what to say."

"It's going to be a very difficult decision if I'm offered the job. I still feel I'll be serving the Lord but in a very different way."

"Will you be giving sermons on the radio?" Jane was sure he would be effective. He certainly was inspiring at Grace Chapel.

"No, I would be working behind the scenes as a producer."

"Everyone in the congregation would hate to see you go. You've come to mean so much to us."

"No one is irreplaceable." He smiled weakly. "I would miss you and your sisters and the many others who've been so kind to me, but it may be time to move on."

"I guess if you have an opportunity to spread the gospel at a wider level, we can't be selfish," she said sadly.

"No one would ever accuse you or your sisters of that. I don't know what will come of the interview. If I am offered a position, I'll have to give it prayerful consideration."

"I hope you're not considering this because you're unhappy at Grace Chapel," Jane said in a worried tone.

"No, certainly not. I appreciate the time I've spent here. I've come to think of the congregation as my family. My mind is in turmoil about this. Part of me would deeply regret leaving, but sometimes I feel that there's nothing more I can do at Grace Chapel to make a difference."

She shook her head, not understanding what he meant. "No church could ask for more than what you do."

"Did your father ever feel the same way as I do? Did he ever feel a call to serve in another capacity?"

"If he ever did, he didn't share his thoughts with me. Of course, I was the youngest, and I wasn't here in later years. But I think he felt a compelling call to minister to the Grace Chapel congregation and use the church as a base to reach out to others."

"I'm not so confident about my calling," he said softly. "I wonder about my effectiveness here and whether I can better serve in some other capacity."

"Kenneth, no one could possibly provide greater spiritual leadership than you do. You've earned the trust of the whole congregation. You carry your mission into the community whenever possible. Look at your grief-counseling work at the Potterston Hospital. How many lives have you turned around through that?"

He shook his head.

"I cherish all the friends I've made here. If I do leave, it won't be because of any dissatisfaction on my part. There are so many factors in the decision that I'm still groping for an answer. I pray that when the time comes, I'll heed the calling of the Lord."

"I wish I knew how to be of help."

"Nothing has been decided. It's possible that I won't be offered the position."

He took his first sip of the cooling tea. "If I am, however, and I decide to accept it, I don't want it to come as a surprise to you. But I would appreciate it if you don't mention it to anyone outside your family. I'm sure your sisters will be discreet."

He didn't need to ask. The last thing Jane wanted was to cause distress by suggesting that Grace Chapel could lose its minister.

"I should leave now," he said. "I hope you'll pray for me."

"Of course, but I'll be praying that you stay."

He smiled broadly for the first time.

"We'll get at the rocker soon," he promised. "I do my best thinking when I'm working with my hands."

"I know exactly what you mean," she said, glad to see him off on a positive note.

Jane walked with him to the front door, saddened to think he was leaving for a job interview. He was such a personable, intelligent man. It seemed unlikely that he would be turned down, especially since this was his second invitation to talk about the position.

She went into the kitchen to do some chores, but she was so distracted that she managed to spill flour into one of the burner wells she'd just cleaned.

How might she tell her sisters? Alice would be terribly distressed. It had been a bit hard for her to get used to someone besides their father heading up the congregation, but now she was one of Rev. Thompson's staunchest supporters. Louise would take the news as calmly as she always did, but she would be heartsick to lose him.

Jane decided to wait a bit before mentioning it to either of them, but she fervently hoped that something would happen to keep Rev. Thompson from leaving. He was more than a spiritual mentor to her. He'd given renewed heart and purpose to the congregation after their long-time minister's death. If he left, he would leave a void that would be very difficult to fill.

Had her father ever thought of leaving Grace Chapel for other challenges? Had he ever thought of going on to something else after years of preaching and serving in Acorn Hill? She didn't know, but Alice might. Alice had been especially close to him in his later years, when Jane and Louise were gone. Still, Jane was hesitant to ask. She didn't want to upset her sister if their pastor should ultimately decide not to leave.

At times like this she knew what a great gift prayer was. She could share her anxieties with the Lord, and somehow He always offered guidance.

Chapter  Five

Jane came downstairs Thursday morning with absolutely no idea what to prepare for breakfast. She rarely experienced such a lack of inspiration. Usually she knew exactly what to fix and, more often than not, she made some preparations the previous evening.

Her lapse was easily explained. She'd been so concerned about the prospect of Rev. Thompson's taking a different position that she'd forgotten about everything else.

This was a bad morning to fall down on her job. The easy-to-please elderly couple had left, but now she was hostess to four men on their way to an antique car rally. One of their friends had recommended Grace Chapel Inn as a good stopping place, so they'd booked all four guest rooms.

When they first arrived early Wednesday evening, it had been fun to see them pull up in front of the inn in cars from a bygone era. The oldest was a Model T Ford, looking as shiny as the day it had rolled off the assembly line. The latest was a Studebaker, a car Jane had forgotten ever existed.

The men, ranging in age from the midforties to a gray-bearded driver who could have been sixty or older, were dressed according to the vehicles they owned, making them an unusually colorful group of guests. They couldn't have been more courteous, and the sisters soon heard more about their trip. Gary, the tall, lanky leader, had organized the tour from Ohio to the rally in Rhode Island, a long trip for their well-restored autos and one they were taking in small stages. He was an attorney in Cleveland, and his traveling friends included a college professor, a dentist and a pharmacist.

They were quiet, cooperative guests, but Jane expected especially hungry diners for breakfast. One of them, whose acquaintance had stayed at the inn, had talked up the inn's food as they were registering. How could she have let the planning slide this way?

Of course, there was no reason to panic. They'd requested breakfast at seven thirty, so she had more than enough time to come up with something tasty. The fridge and freezer were well stocked, and she hit on the idea of providing a smorgasbord instead of the usual individual presentations. A coffeemaker on the buffet would allow them to help themselves to an unlimited amount of the beverage during the course of the meal, and they could fill their plates as often as they liked.

Eggs were always popular, and her special scrambles were especially well regarded. She chopped onions, green peppers and mushrooms, then browned them before adding the eggs. A dusting of parmesan and parsley before serving topped off the presentation. That dish was easily prepared, and she could keep it on a warming tray on the buffet.

Would they like grits? She would prepare that dish in addition to homemade buttermilk biscuits. There was time to mix up a batch if she hurried. The grits and biscuits were best with some redeye gravy. She could add ham bits from the freezer. Jane liked to add a touch of coffee to enrich this Southern favorite.

Her mind was in a whirl, reminding her of experiences as a restaurant chef trying to keep up with customers' orders on a busy day.

"Anything I can do to help?" Alice asked as she came into the kitchen.

"Lots!" Jane said gratefully. "I suspect our guests may have substantial appetites this morning. I'm doing a buffet. Would you mind taking care of the fruit? Make a big tray using everything you can find in the fridge."

"I can do that," Alice said, sounding a bit relieved that her task was simple.

"Oh, put a dish of cottage cheese in the center. It would be great if you make the coffee too."

Jane lined up her big skillet and the other pans she would need, then gave some thought to a meat dish. It was flattering to have guests who'd been encouraged by someone else who'd stayed there, but it also put pressure on her to provide the kind of hearty breakfast that would appeal to her diners.

"Canadian bacon!" she said, startling Alice who was peeling an orange. "That's what I'll fry. It will make a nice accompaniment to the eggs."

If Alice was surprised by her sister's spur-of-the-minute menu planning, she didn't say so.

By seven thirty, Jane was satisfied with the buffet. She'd browned some packaged sausages and had Alice slice oatmeal bread. Then she warmed a loaf of her homemade caraway-rye and placed fresh creamery butter and homemade raspberry jam on the side.

The guests came down as a group, talking a language that was foreign to Jane. Conversation about carburetors, gears and hand-cranking came to a halt when the men descended on the buffet.

"I'll be a monkey's uncle," the gray-bearded man said. "Don't tell me that's redeye gravy. I haven't had any since I was in short pants. My dear, if that's as good as my granny used to make, I'm gonna marry you."

Jane laughed off his enthusiasm, but she was glad her impromptu buffet was a hit. In fact, she had to heat up the skillet a second time to make more eggs. She had so much fun watching a group of really enthusiastic eaters devour practically everything in sight that she temporarily forgot her concern about Rev. Thompson's job interview.

"Well, that was a first," Alice said when their contented guests had left.

"Yes, imagine if Grace Chapel Inn becomes a trendy place for antique auto enthusiasts to stay," Jane said, still grinning from the good-natured praise the men had heaped on her.

"I don't mean the guests," Alice said. "I mean, you didn't seem at all yourself this morning. Usually you know exactly what you plan to serve well in advance. Today you seemed to be making it up as you went along."

"It was fun, though, wasn't it? Next time I'll know exactly what to serve a group of hearty eaters like them. I gave the man with the gray beard my recipe for redeye gravy. He said he'd like to try cooking it for himself."

∞

Louise was sorry to have missed helping with Jane's successful buffet, but she'd promised to give a lesson that morning. She tried to be flexible, knowing most of her pupils were involved in activities that made demands on their limited time, and this morning's student had the school's permission to fit in her lesson.

She heard the old automobiles leave while she was in the parlor with her student. In fact, the whole town had probably noticed their colorful departure. They'd been ideal guests according to her sisters, vocally appreciative of everything the inn had to offer. Louise never ceased to be amazed by the interesting people who came to their bed-and-breakfast.

When the lesson was finished, Louise made her way to the kitchen to join her sisters. A moment later Ethel called out from the entryway, "Good morning! Is anyone here?"

"In the kitchen, Aunt Ethel," Alice answered. Ethel

hurried into the kitchen, looking frazzled. Her hair was stuck together on one side and standing out on the other as though she'd bolted from her bed without bothering to comb it. She wasn't wearing makeup, which was odd, but her cheeks were flushed with excitement. Strangest of all, she was wearing a pink floral wrapper with her nightgown showing at the hem.

"Is something wrong?" Louise quickly asked.

"Yes, very, very wrong!"

Ethel sat on the nearest chair and caught her breath. Without being asked, Jane got a glass of water and held it out for her aunt. After several swallows, Ethel seemed ready to tell them what was happening.

"I just had a telephone call from Florence Simpson, and I can't believe what she had to say."

Louise's opinion was that it was better not to put complete belief in everything Florence said, because she enjoyed gossip as much as Ethel did, but Louise didn't want to be unkind and say so.

"She has a cleaning lady from Potterston who also works once a week for our own Rev. Thompson," Ethel said, still a bit breathless from hurrying to the inn. "Florence has had her working extra days to do some spring housekeeping chores, and you'll never believe what she told Florence. Our pastor may be planning to leave us."

"What are you talking about?" Alice asked a trifle impatiently.

"I mean to say, he took time off in the middle of the week to go out of town. The cleaning lady saw an envelope from a church radio station in his trash basket."

"That doesn't mean a thing," Louise said, not at all liking third-hand gossip. "He probably gets all kinds of mail."

"No, this was different," Ethel insisted. "I know it was wrong of her, but the cleaning lady—I can't tell you her name because I promised Florence I wouldn't—also saw a crumpled letter and gave it a . . . passing glance. He has an appointment this very day."

"You're both making too much of this," Alice insisted. "It's terrible of that cleaning person to go through the trash and spread rumors about what she finds. You really shouldn't tell another soul about this, Aunt Ethel. There's probably some perfectly reasonable explanation that has nothing to do with Kenneth's leaving Acorn Hill."

"Florence was positive. He's away interviewing for a job. I hate to think he might want to leave us," Ethel said excitedly. "He's such a wonderful preacher. It would be a terrible loss to everyone in the congregation if he goes."

"Yes," Alice agreed, "but that doesn't excuse prying and spreading rumors."

Louise was surprised at Alice. It was unlike her to scold their somewhat flighty aunt, but Alice did feel strongly about the negative effects of gossip. She worked with life-and-death situations at the hospital, where the patients' families could be terribly alarmed by an idle rumor.

"I think it would be best if you put it out of your mind and didn't mention it to anyone else," Alice said in a kinder voice.

"Yes, I suppose you're right," Ethel said, sounding deflated. "Even Florence wants to keep a lid on things. She asked me not to tell anyone besides you."

Louise smiled, knowing her aunt's relationship with Florence was sometimes rocky. They both loved to gossip, but that wasn't always a good basis for friendship.

"Dear, look at me! I came out in my nightclothes. What will people think of me?"

"I doubt anyone saw you," Alice assured her, "and unless you go to town dressed that way, no one will."

"Well, I'm not about to go to town, but I better get back home."

"Be careful not to trip in your mules," Louise warned. "Would you like me to walk back with you?"

"No, thank you," Ethel said, sounding a bit miffed at the suggestion that she needed an escort. "I'm still quite capable of walking home unaided."

"I'm sure you are," Louise agreed.

"I'm not going to tell anyone but you about Rev. Thompson," she said as a parting shot. "I know to be discreet about church affairs."

"I'm sure you do," Alice said. "We'll keep this among ourselves."

When their aunt was gone, Louise noticed that Jane had been unusually quiet. In fact, she'd not reacted in any way to Ethel's news.

"You're not upset by Florence's gossip, are you?" Louise asked.

"There's something I have to tell you," she said solemnly.

"What's wrong?" Alice asked, hovering near the table.

"You'd better sit down."

Louise had a bad feeling about her sister's tone.

"I don't like keeping secrets from the two of you," Jane began, "but I thought this one would only distress you. Kenneth is interviewing for a position in the church's radio ministry."

"He's really interested in leaving Grace Chapel?" Alice sounded shocked.

"He hasn't had a job offer yet, and he hasn't decided whether to accept if he does get one."

"Oh dear. That would be an awful loss to the chapel. He's doing such a wonderful job. I never thought anyone could replace Father, but Kenneth has come to mean so much to all of us," Alice said.

"Yes," Jane said sadly, "but he seems to feel it may be time to accept the challenge of serving the Lord in a new capacity."

"Will he be preaching on the air?" Louise asked.

"No, the job involves working behind the scenes."

"It would be a shame if his voice is heard no more," Louise said. "He's so effective as a leader in the congregation. Of course, we can't be selfish if he has a call to broaden the scope of his work."

"I'm not sure what his duties as a radio producer would

be, but I'm afraid he'll squander his talent for leading people to Jesus," Jane said. "Did Father ever have doubts about remaining with his congregation?"

Louise didn't have an answer to that, but Alice immediately spoke up.

"I think that late in life he worried that he was getting too old to carry on the Lord's work at the chapel. He didn't doubt his mission, only his ability to fulfill it in later years."

"He retired at eighty-two," Jane said. "He deserved some rest."

"He continued giving sermons and reaching out to people until his death," Alice reminded them. "He saw faith as a journey with obstacles to overcome, not a static condition. That's the best answer I can give you."

"It's a good one," Jane said thoughtfully. "I am sorry for keeping this from you. Kenneth was willing to have you know, but I didn't want you to worry needlessly. He may decide to stay even if he's offered the position."

"You did the right thing," Alice assured her. "I'm worried that the rumor will spread even if Aunt Ethel keeps quiet. We can't depend on Florence's discretion, I'm afraid."

"Or the housekeeper's." Louise frowned. "She's already demonstrated that."

"This does put my concern about chaperoning a class trip in perspective," Alice said.

"It's still a big responsibility," Louise assured her. "And speaking of responsibilities, I'd better go over to Nine Lives to see how Sarah is handling things. She's a sweet girl but not always inclined to be sensible, I'm afraid."

"Maybe I'll go over and have another word with Aunt Ethel," Jane said. "If Kenneth does feel compelled to leave, he should be allowed to announce it in his own way."

"It may be too late," Alice said, "but Aunt Ethel will need comforting. She probably feels bad about spreading Florence's gossip now that she's had time to think about it. I don't suppose it would do any good to speak to Florence."

"No," Louise said emphatically, seconded by Jane. "If we make any kind of fuss about it, she'll be even more convinced that she has big news to tell. To be fair to Kenneth, we have to give him space until we know what he's going to do."

"Shouldn't we talk to him? Tell him how much he's appreciated here?" Alice asked.

"I don't know what we could possibly say if he's wrestling with making a decision to follow a different path. It's something we need to take to the Lord in prayer," Louise said.

"Whatever he decides, we'll have to try to accept it with good grace and pray that it's best for him," Alice said. "But I would hate to lose him."

Louise left for Nine Lives. There was nothing else she could contribute about their pastor, and she did feel a bit uneasy about leaving Sarah alone in the bookstore all day. She hurried toward town, hoping she would find Sarah in the store.

From the outside, the shop looked like a tranquil oasis for book lovers. A woman outside was looking at the window display, but she moved on before Louise got there. Sarah had replaced the somewhat tired silk flowers in the baskets with bunches of daffodils. The arrangements were a bit skimpy for the size of the containers, but Louise was pleased that she'd taken the initiative.

She noticed Mr. Trotty's bike chained to the outside bench, so when she went inside, she wasn't surprised to see him once again studying a page in a fishing book. What she hadn't expected was chaos. Everywhere she looked, the floor was covered with piles of books.

She made her way past stacks of cookbooks teetering in precarious towers and nearly tripped over a small pile of novels left right in the center of the store. Louise was astonished.

"Sarah!"

"Oh, good morning, Mrs. Smith," she said, stepping out from the back room with a can of soda in hand. "Ms. Reed doesn't like me to eat or drink in front, so I went in the back for a soft drink."

"What on earth happened here?"

"Oh, I'm dusting. It's part of my job."

"But why take so many books off the shelves? Customers can't browse with things in this condition."

"It's so hard to keep track of where I've dusted. Every time I stop to help a customer, I forget where I left off. I thought if I put them on the floor and return them as I finish dusting each one, I won't get confused."

"No one can look at them this way. Viola keeps them organized on the shelves so they're easy to locate."

"I'm dusting as fast as I can. Oh, good morning, Mr. Trotty. I thought that was you who came in. Did you get the new tire for your bike?"

He mumbled something without looking up from the book.

"Anyway, Mrs. Smith, it's not as if the store is ever crowded. If someone wants a book, I can point them to the right pile."

"Sarah, this won't do. We have to put the books back as quickly as possible. Imagine how bad you would feel if someone tripped over them."

"I didn't think of that. Don't you think the piles are pretty easy to see?"

"Please, I'll help you."

"Can we dust as we go? I couldn't find the feather duster, so I've been using a cloth. I can get one for you too."

"Thank you, Sarah, but let's forget dusting for now. The books have to be shelved as quickly as possible."

She started replacing cookbooks on the appropriate shelf, but Sarah just stared at the piles as if lost in thought.

"Aren't you going to help me?" Louise asked, trying not to show exasperation.

"I forget where this one goes," Sarah confessed, picking up the top book from an especially high stack. "It's about building a picnic table and stuff. Does it go in gardening or home improvement? It doesn't have anything to do with a house, and the table wouldn't necessarily go in a garden. It could be in a park or on a deck."

"Look at the rest of the stack," Louise said, calling on deep reserves of patience. "Are they gardening or home improvement books?"

"Not exactly."

Louise walked over to check for herself. The picnic table book topped a pile of mystery novels and bestsellers. Returning all the books to the shelf was going to be a huge job.

"Tell you what. You hand me the books, and I'll find the appropriate shelf," she said.

"I was hoping to arrange them by the color of the covers. You know, all the reds together, all the greens together, all the yellows and so on. It will make the shelves into a work of art."

"No one will be able to find what they want."

"I didn't think of that. You see, Mrs. Smith, I'm really not cut out for bookstore work. Maybe I should quit now."

"Don't even think of it!" Louise said as sternly as possible. "Viola is counting on you. You don't want to let her down, do you?"

"No, she's done so much for me."

"Then let's forget you even thought of it and get these books back in place."

"I can lend a hand," Mr. Trotty said in a raspy voice, replacing the fishing book in exactly the right space on the shelf.

Before Louise could say that it was too much to ask of him, Sarah enthusiastically accepted his offer.

"That would be wonderful, Mr. Trotty. I'm afraid I've jumbled them up more than I intended."

The small, white-haired man only grunted and picked up the closest pile of books. With only a scant glance, he divided them between the child care and inspirational shelves. Louise began shelving as quickly as possible, but it soon became clear that Mr. Trotty was working much faster. He had an uncanny knack for organizing them in the right categories.

It was hard work, but the piles gradually shrank until

only a few books remained to be shelved. Soon their volunteer put the last volume in place and started to leave the store.

"Mr. Trotty, thank you so much," Louise called after him.

Sarah followed him outside, and Louise could see her thanking him profusely.

"He enjoyed that," she said when she came back inside.

"Yes, he did seem to."

"He was a librarian at a university in Maine before he retired. Can you believe I was only a baby when he stopped working and moved here to be near his sister's family? His sister passed away a few years ago. A niece looks in on him from time to time, but he gets lonely. Poor guy, he must be bored, just riding around town on his bike every day. He loves fishing, but his niece is afraid to have him out in a boat alone, so he just comes here and looks at pictures of fish."

In spite of the fiasco with the books, Louise was impressed with Sarah's people skills. She'd gotten to know something about Mr. Trotty and sympathized with his loneliness. To most people, he was just an eccentric senior citizen who rode his bike in all types of weather. Louise was ashamed of herself for not seeing him as a person in need of companionship and a sense of purpose. She made a mental note to mention him to Rev. Thompson, then remembered that the minister might be leaving them.

She took a deep breath and turned her attention to the bookstore.

After she did the accounting and took yesterday's receipts out of the safe to deposit at the bank, she waited until Sarah finished helping a customer.

Part of her wanted to rebuke Sarah for taking down all the books and warn her not to make any other changes in the way Viola ran the store, but she'd learned from years of teaching piano that scolding was rarely effective. She needed to focus on what she expected from Sarah.

"We should talk about the book group," she said when Sarah was alone in the front of the shop.

"I've had a wonderful idea for the refreshments. Ms. Reed said it was up to me to come up with something nice, and I know just what to serve—plum pudding and grog. Doesn't that sound like something Scrooge would love?"

"Yes, a Victorian touch would be fine. But do you know what grog is?"

"Oh, something to drink. I'll look it up on the Internet."

"I think you'll find that it's a rum drink served to sailors in the British Navy in the days of sailing ships. I'm afraid it wouldn't be appropriate for the book group."

"I suppose tea would be British enough." Sarah sounded a bit disappointed.

"But we can look into plum pudding," Louise said, trying to sound positive. "I don't think it's something you can buy at the bakery though. It will have to be homemade."

"Oh, that's no problem. I'll make it at my aunt's."

"Have you ever made it?" Louise expected a negative response.

"No, but I've made brownies. How hard can plum pudding be?"

"I've only tasted it once or twice, but I think it involves a long process. I know it has to be steamed for quite a while."

Louise knew Sarah would need help, but her conscience was at war. She was torn between imposing on overworked Jane or allowing Sarah to engineer a culinary disaster. She looked at the bookshelves, reorganized with no small amount of work, and decided Jane would forgive her.

"My sister is a professional chef," she said guardedly. "Maybe you could consult with her before you firm up your plans."

"Great! She can give me some hints."

"She does all the cooking for our bed-and-breakfast, so I'll have to check with her to find a good time for you to talk to her. Maybe you could stop by the inn after work someday soon. You know where it is, don't you?"

"Oh, yes, that big spooky-looking house down the road. I'd love to go there. I've wondered if it's haunted."

"It certainly is not," Louise said firmly, not wanting to get into fanciful theories about ghosts.

She thought the inn was warmly welcoming, not in the least forbidding. She was a bit miffed by Sarah's comment, but she was learning that the girl could be considerate one minute and thoughtless the next. Sarah tended to blurt out whatever was in her head at the moment. The girl probably had no idea that her comment about the inn might not be appreciated by one of its owners.

"I'll mention your idea about plum pudding to my sister, and we'll find a time when you can come talk to her about it."

"Cool! That gives me another idea. Maybe we can dim the lights when the book group meets here, make the place seem more Victorian and spooky. Weren't there a bunch of ghosts in that book they're reading? We can decorate with cobwebs and hang sheets with painted ghostly faces in the window. Candlelight, that's what we need. No electric lights, just candles."

"The fire marshal would have a problem with that. Why don't you concentrate on the refreshments and let me worry about the ambiance?"

"Music!" Sarah blurted out as though inspired. "You teach piano. Do you have a tape with some really eerie music we can play in the background?"

Louise groaned inwardly and fervently hoped that Sarah wouldn't decide to read the book. She absolutely wasn't going to allow rattling chains or cardboard gravestones at a meeting of book lovers. There would be no theatrical tricks on her watch.

Chapter Six

Alice stopped in the office of Acorn Hill Elementary School Friday morning, a requirement for all visitors, and signed a guest book indicating that she would be visiting Vera's fifth graders. A woman working at one of the desks gave her directions to the classroom.

This wasn't the building where Alice and Louise had learned their ABCs. That two-story, late-Victorian structure had been replaced while Alice was still in high school, but she remembered well the long, narrow windows that had seemed so unusual on her first day in kindergarten. She had memories of blackboards that were really black, not green or white like modern ones, and scarred wooden desks with holes that had held a bottle of ink, relics of the days before ballpoints.

Her fondest memory of elementary school involved Mrs. Bestor, the third-grade teacher. Everyone thought she was the prettiest and nicest teacher in the school. Alice could still visualize her, dark brown hair piled high on her head, always wearing pretty bright-colored blouses. Her voice was soft and lilting, and she often led the children in songs of their choice. She never spoke in anger or kept children in from recess as punishment, yet her class was known as the best behaved. Alice tried to remember what had given

Mrs. Bestor that special magic with young people, then decided it must have been the love she showed for them.

She wouldn't be surprised if Vera, too, earned a place in her students' fondest memories. Every child who was fortunate enough to have her as a teacher became one of her own, and she cared for them with a combination of practical good sense and deep concern for their needs. Although this was the first time Alice had visited Vera's classroom, she had followed her friend's career and knew how much the community valued her.

Knocking softly on the closed door, Alice hoped that her visit wouldn't disrupt a lesson. Vera had invited her to come whenever it was convenient, and Alice opted for a time before the morning recess.

One of the students opened the door, a tall slender boy with an unruly mop of thick mahogany hair and bangs that reached the top of his narrow glasses.

"Good morning, Miss Alice," Vera called out from in front of the chalkboard, using the name they had decided was most appropriate for a chaperone. "That's Erik, one of the boys who will be in your group on the trip."

"Hello, Erik. I'm pleased to meet you."

"Hello." He drifted back to his seat at one of the tables, apparently a young man of few words.

"Sit anywhere you see a chair," Vera invited. "We're just finishing math."

Vera continued the lesson, writing bold numerals on the board. Alice glanced around and couldn't help comparing the classroom to the austere rooms in the old elementary school. Instead of bare floorboards worn down by generations of young feet, the pale beige tile was only lightly scuffed. The tables were metal with light-green Formica tops and had room for six chairs at each. Corkboards covered all the reachable wall space, and Vera had loaded them with collages of student art, charts, pictures and projects. Alice could understand why the Humbert home was swamped with stacks and boxes of her teaching materials. The classroom didn't begin to have enough storage for her huge collection, and she used her own home to make her classroom a pleasant learning center.

The biggest change from Alice's school days was the use of computers. She counted five in the classroom and spotted a schedule for student use. When she was in fifth grade, it was a big treat to have a movie in the room. They even had a student club—all boys if she remembered correctly—who had the privilege of being trained to run the projector. The films were usually black and white, and scratched from years of use, not to mention dated.

The math lesson ended, and the students began purposeful movements around the room. That was different from her day when students had to stay seated at their desks unless they were given permission to get up. She almost envied today's pupils, until she remembered how much more they had to learn, especially when it came to science and computers. When she thought back to her father's stories about the one-room school he'd attended through the sixth grade, the contrast was amazing. His lone teacher had only needed a short course of study at a normal school to qualify for her seemingly impossible job of instructing six grades at once.

"Before we begin our science reports," Vera said, "I would like to introduce Miss Alice Howard. Thanks to her, we have enough chaperones to go on our trip to Philadelphia. Besides Erik, Matt will be in your group."

"Hi, Matt," Alice said, nodding at a tall, grinning boy whose hair stood up in spikes.

"And Andrew."

A fair, short-haired boy nodded without looking up from the computer where he was intently studying the screen.

"It's Andrew's turn on the number-one computer," Vera said by way of explanation for his preoccupation. "Then there's Alex. He just moved here from Virginia."

She nodded at a boy with dark, mischievous eyes, coffee-colored skin and hair clipped short.

"Chad is the fifth boy in your group. He's absent today."

Vera gave a little shrug that Alice couldn't interpret. Was the fifth boy likely to be a problem? She made a mental note to ask her friend before the field trip.

After observing for a while longer, Alice thanked the class for letting her visit and said how much she was looking forward to their trip. Then she left for home. Because she would be gone all day Monday, she wanted to complete some household chores at the inn today.

Louise wanted to show confidence in Sarah, but she couldn't forget the fiasco with the books the day before. After breakfast, she prepared for her afternoon piano lessons and paid a few bills for the inn, but she couldn't get Nine Lives out of her mind.

Viola called shortly after the surgery to report that her aunt's procedure had been successful but, given her age, the elderly woman would be in the hospital at least until Monday. After that, Viola wanted to help her at home for a few days, which meant she definitely wouldn't be back for the book group scheduled next week on the first Thursday of May.

Louise assured her that all was well at the shop, hoping that she wasn't stretching the truth. Just as Jane had tried to shield them from worrying about Rev. Thompson, she saw no reason to alarm Viola with tales of Sarah's unusual take on running a bookstore. It was enough for Viola to be concerned about the elderly relative she was so fond of.

"What are your plans for the day?" Jane asked when Louise came into the kitchen for a midmorning cup of tea.

"I'm debating whether to check on Sarah at Nine Lives this morning or wait until later in the afternoon. I want her to think I trust her, but I'm uneasy about what she'll try next.

I suggested that she use any spare moments to look for a plum pudding recipe on the Internet."

"I forgot that you mentioned plum pudding. That's something I've never made," Jane said pensively. "You said she wants to serve it to the book group next week?"

"Yes. Is it something you'd like to try?"

"Possibly."

"Would you—no, it's too much to ask."

"Do you want me to help her with it?"

"You're so busy I hate to ask. Working with Sarah is challenging."

"She sounds enthusiastic."

"She is that," Louise said a bit dryly.

"Tell you what. Have her come see me, and I'll go over the recipe with her. If it looks like more than she can handle, I'll help. It would be a shame if things aren't nice for the book group. Viola is so enthusiastic about it."

"If you're sure you don't mind."

"It could be fun to make authentic plum pudding," Jane said optimistically, "but it wouldn't be fair to make Sarah drive home to Potterston, then come back here after dinner to see me. When it's convenient for her to come after the bookstore closes at five, I'll fix something for our meal that can be in the oven ahead of time."

Louise thanked her sister, left the inn and walked slowly toward the bookstore. The sky was drab gray, and she carried her umbrella in anticipation of a downpour before she got home. If everything was going smoothly at Nine Lives, she would take yesterday's receipts from the safe and put together the deposit, then go to the bank and trust Sarah to lock up at the end of the day. It was a big *if*.

The first person she saw when she entered the store was Mr. Trotty but, surprisingly, he wasn't studying a page in the usual fishing book. In fact, he wasn't reading at all. He was standing beside a corrugated cardboard box filled with hardcover volumes and was methodically putting them on a shelf.

"Good morning, Mr. Trotty." Louise decided not to ask him what he was doing. No doubt Sarah could explain.

The assistant was nowhere in sight, so Louise went to the back room and found her hunched over the computer. Tess was curled up in her lap. The instant Sarah noticed her, she made the screen go blank.

"Is there something I should know?" Louise steeled herself for another of the girl's unusual ideas.

"I'm sorry, I shouldn't have been playing solitaire on the computer, but the time goes so slowly."

"I meant about Mr. Trotty."

"Oh."

"He seems to be stocking the shelves."

"Well, technically, it's my job, but he really got a kick out of helping yesterday. I didn't think it would hurt to let him do a little work today. He doesn't want to be paid or anything. He just wants to feel useful."

How could Louise argue against a kindness? She didn't know what to say. "Do you think it would be all right with Viola?" she finally asked

"I didn't think of that."

"It's nice of you to be so thoughtful, but I'm not sure it's a good idea."

Louise tried to decide whether it really was all right. She wondered if Sarah was playing Tom Sawyer, getting someone else to do her work while she played games on the computer. On the other hand, the man did seem happy. Would Viola want him to continue helping? If she didn't, would she be too tenderhearted to forbid it? Some of the shelves were high, and Mr. Trotty was frail and elderly. What if he hurt himself stocking them?

Common sense suggested that she call Viola that evening and let her decide, but Louise didn't want her friend to be anxious about the way Sarah was handling her duties at the store.

"Maybe you'd better not give him jobs where he has to climb on the stool," Louise suggested.

"Okay," Sarah agreed cheerfully. "By the way, we're out of quarters and nearly out of dimes. Do you want to go for change, or should I do it while you watch the store?"

"Why don't you go? I'll make up a deposit from yesterday's receipts, and you can use part of them to get a supply of change. It will only take me a couple of minutes." Louise hoped that the girl might be less restless after a brisk walk over to the bank.

Sarah's responsibilities included putting the day's receipts in the safe every evening after closing, leaving only a set amount in the cash drawer for the next day's trade. When Louise took out the cloth bank sack, she found a jumble of checks and wrinkled bills in no particular order. It appeared that business had been good the previous day, so it took her a little while to sort out the receipts and prepare a deposit slip. She refilled Tess' water and food while she was at it.

"What should I do with the box?" Mr. Trotty asked, coming part way into the back area.

He'd already flattened it for recycling, but Louise didn't know the procedure.

"Sarah can tell you."

"She's not here."

"Oh! Well, please just leave it against the wall there, Mr. Trotty. I'll be right back."

He stepped aside as Louise hurried out to the front to confirm Sarah's absence. How could it be possible? Sarah had deserted her job again.

Louise went to the front door and out to the street where the sun was breaking through the clouds. Sarah had wandered down to the town hall, but she wasn't alone. A landscaping truck was parked on the street, and a young man in a green T-shirt with a company logo had abandoned his shovel and clippers to chat with her. Even from a distance, Louise could see that he was handsome with sun-bleached hair caught in a tail, and skin already lightly bronzed from working outside. She could understand why two young people would rather visit with each other than do their jobs, but she worried that Sarah might leave the store untended again when she wasn't there.

Louise felt awkward standing outside in her blue shirt-dress and sensible walking shoes, imagining that the young people saw her as an obstacle to their budding friendship. Certainly she hadn't signed on to be a chaperone, but Viola was trusting Sarah to run the store.

Two women, a mother and daughter whom Louise knew by sight, went into the store, nodding at her but looking a little puzzled by her vigil on the sidewalk. She followed them and spent the next ten minutes or so helping them find a book on camping for the younger one's son. By the time they left, so had Mr. Trotty, and Sarah still hadn't returned. She must have assumed that Louise had time to mind the store while she socialized. Or, more likely, she was too distracted by the young man to give it a thought.

When she finally returned, Sarah's cheeks were flushed and her eyes sparkled.

"Buck Diesel wants to see me this Saturday, Mrs. Smith. Isn't that exciting?"

Louise shook her head, regretting the lecture she had to give.

"That's very nice, Sarah, but you can't leave the store untended. You promised Viola that you would be responsible for it."

"You were here," she said apologetically, as if realizing for the first time that she might have done something wrong.

"Yes, and you were going to go to the bank for change when I finished the receipts, remember? I'm trying to help as much as I can, but I do have other responsibilities—the inn and my lessons. You'll have to check with me if you want to leave the store."

"I'm really sorry. I just stuck my head out for some air,

and I saw the truck parked by the town hall. It's not very far from here."

"Please, tell me you won't do it again."

"I promise. I will stay in the store unless you're free to watch it."

Louise didn't doubt her sincerity, but would the young woman remember her promise the next time she was tempted to wander off? She sighed and decided to take care of making the deposit and getting the change herself.

"One more thing," Louise said. "Have you found a plum pudding recipe to serve the book group?"

"Oh, I meant to do that." Sarah was again apologetic. "If I'm not busy this afternoon, I'll check on the Internet."

"I have a suggestion. My sister Jane was quite interested in your idea. No doubt she can easily find a recipe in her collection of cookbooks. She's willing to give you a few pointers if you would like to drop by the inn sometime."

"I'd love to. I've always wanted to see the inside of a haunted—I mean, an old house like yours. Is it okay if I stop by after work today?"

"After work would probably be fine," Louise said, "but it would be best if we call the inn first, just to be sure."

∞

Jane noticed that Louise sounded a bit edgy when she mentioned Sarah Lister's request to visit the inn that day. After years of working with piano students, her sister had a real knack for getting along with young people, so it seemed unlikely that Viola's assistant was the cause of her agitation.

Jane pulled out several books and soon found a plum pudding recipe that reminded her of the delicious one a friend had given her as a Christmas gift quite a few years ago. She thought it would do nicely.

She had just placed a salmon loaf and scalloped potatoes in the oven when she heard the clunk of footsteps in the entryway. She went out to see a tall, thin girl in wooden-soled wedges, a short pink skirt and a black top that didn't quite meet the waistband of the skirt.

"Mrs. Smith told me to walk right in," she said a bit uncertainly. "I hope it's okay."

"Yes, the door is always open for our guests," Jane said, feeling a bit dwarfed by the lanky girl, although she was tall herself by most standards. "You must be Sarah Lister. I'm Jane Howard."

"That's me. I can't tell you how excited I am to be inside your inn. Would it be asking too much to show me around? I get shivers just thinking about all the people who lived here in the past."

Jane was surprised by the request, but she was used to visitors.

"All right," she agreed. "This is where we register our guests and keep the reservation book."

"Have people died in any of the rooms?"

"Not that I know of."

"But what about the people who lived here ages ago?"

"The house has been in our family for quite a few years. I'm not certain who built it, but it was always a residence until we opened the bed-and-breakfast. This is the library."

"Why does it have a sign on the door?"

"We thought it would be a nice memorial to our father. It was his favorite room, and he wrote all his sermons here."

Sarah glanced into the library, the parlor, the dining room and the living room, but Jane thought that she showed little interest in any of them, considering her request to see the house.

"Your inn has such a special aura," she said. "Do you think I could go upstairs?"

"Our guest rooms are on the second floor," Jane explained, leading the way. "Two of them are occupied, so I can't open them for you. No one is assigned to the Garden Room, so you can take a peek in there."

Sarah didn't comment on the garden theme in the room

with the lovely rosewood bedroom suite. In fact, she didn't react in any way to the décor. Jane thought her indifference was somewhat odd. Jane had served as decorator during the renovations, and although she wasn't fishing for compliments, she was surprised that the girl showed no interest in what she was seeing.

"What's on the third floor?" she asked. "I don't think I've ever been in a house with three floors."

"Three stories and an attic," Jane said. "My sisters and I have rooms on the next floor. You can see mine if you like, but I wouldn't feel right taking you into my sisters' bedrooms."

Again Jane led the way, opening the door to her room.

"It's very modern, isn't it?" Sarah said, looking at the eggplant-colored walls and blond Danish furniture. "Not that it isn't very pretty. I just wasn't expecting anything so up-to-date."

Was that a compliment? Jane wasn't sure because Sarah sounded disappointed.

"Now if you'd like to take a look at our plum pudding recipe," Jane said, "we can go down to the kitchen."

"But I haven't seen the attic." She was standing in the hallway, eyes closed, swaying on her awkward platform shoes.

"There's nothing there but a jumble of trunks, boxes and discarded furniture. You wouldn't be interested in anything there."

"Oh, but I would," Sarah said with surprising urgency. "I'd love to experience every inch of the house."

"The steps are pretty steep. I wouldn't want you to trip in your high platforms."

"No problem." She slipped out of them. "I'll be careful, and I won't touch a thing."

"Well, watch your step," Jane cautioned, somewhat reluctantly leading the way to the attic and turning on the dim overhead light.

"This is so exciting," she said, again swaying with her eyes closed. "Did anyone ever hide up here?"

"No one over the age of ten," Jane assured her.

"I mean like runaway slaves or fugitives from the law."

"The house isn't old enough to have been a stop on the Underground Railroad, and I very much doubt that the original owners had anything to do with outlaws. Now, let's see about the recipe."

She ushered Sarah back to the main floor and into the kitchen.

"I bet your cellar is spooky," she said.

"Not in the slightest," Jane said, balking at a tour of the basement. "Now, I've made a copy of the plum pudding recipe. It's usually served with hard sauce, so I copied that too."

"Oh, I wonder if hard sauce will work," Sarah said earnestly. "The book people will have to eat without a table. They won't be able to cut anything hard."

"It's only a name for a nice creamy sauce. Here, read this. It's only confectioners' sugar with butter and vanilla."

"Sort of like frosting but juicy?"

"I guess that description works." Jane smiled, more bemused than irritated by Sarah's unusual take on things. "The key to plum pudding is that it has to be steamed."

"Like with a kettle?" Sarah brushed a lock of hair behind her ear and pursed her lips into a cherry-red O.

"No, the mixture is steamed for six hours in a pan of boiling water."

"Doesn't it, you know, turn into soup in the water?"

"Not if one uses a mold with a good cover, one that's waterproof. The water only needs to go halfway up the mold. I've heard of people making individual puddings using canned-goods containers with foil tightly secured on top."

"It sounds complicated." Sarah seemed worried.

"A little," Jane agreed, "but if you take it one step at a time, it should turn out just fine. It's a great idea to serve a Victorian treat to a group discussing Dickens. Let's look at the ingredients you'll need."

"Bread, milk, sugar, eggs," Sarah read. "I can find those at the supermarket. What on earth is suet?"

"Fat."

"Oh, you mean like margarine."

"No, suet is animal fat. In Dickens's time, it probably came from mutton, but you'll have an easier time finding beef suet. Your butcher can help."

"You mean fat like that white stuff on raw meat?" Sarah sounded dismayed. "That sounds gross."

"When it's creamed and combined with the other ingredients, you won't even know it's there," Jane assured her. "Now, are there any other ingredients and directions you don't understand?"

"Mace and citron and figs. There aren't any plums in the recipe. Are you sure this is plum pudding?"

"Quite sure. In olden times, *plum* may have been a name for *fig*. That's only a guess, but I have eaten plum pudding, and it's delicious. Viola will be proud of you for thinking of it."

"Oh no, it has raisins. I loathe raisins. I can't possibly make something that has raisins in it."

"You don't have to make it," Jane said in an understanding voice. "I can see where it's a pretty intimidating recipe. Maybe you should pick up something at the bakery instead."

"No, I said I would make it, and I want to show that I can be depended on. I just hope my aunt will help me. She's still pretty unhappy because I forgot a pan of cookies I'd put in the oven recently, and they turned to charcoal. But I bought her a new baking sheet, so maybe she'll let me in the kitchen again."

Jane had a sinking feeling. There were probably a dozen or more ways for Sarah to turn plum pudding into a culinary disaster. What if she tried to serve a ruined dessert? Viola was so eager for the book group to be a long-lasting success. Mass food poisoning just might have an adverse effect on its future.

"Maybe I should help you." Jane tried not to show her reluctance. "You can make it here."

"That's wonderful! You're just as sweet as your sister. I don't know how I can thank you enough."

"I have a big pot to steam it, and I'll come up with a waterproof mold. Also, I have a good supply of the sugar, salt and spices you'll need. You take care of buying the other ingredients. You'll have better luck shopping in Potterston. Be sure to ask for help at the supermarket if you aren't sure about what to get."

"Thank you, thank you, thank you. I really want this to be nice for Ms. Reed's group." She flung her arms around Jane in a big bear hug. "Just tell me when you want me here with the ingredients."

Jane made arrangements for their cooking date and saw Sarah to the door. Maybe she should have discouraged her from serving a complicated dessert, but she sympathized with Sarah for her ambitious plans. Maybe they would both learn something.

A little later, Louise came into the kitchen to set the table for dinner. Jane told her about Sarah's visit and her offer to help with the plum pudding.

"I hope you don't regret it," Louise said with uncharacteristic pessimism.

"It will be fine. I'll be right beside her to help. What can possibly go wrong? One thing, though—I don't understand why she wanted to see the house, especially the attic. She even wanted to go down to the cellar, but I nixed that."

"The inn is old, so she thinks it must be haunted," Louise explained, rolling her eyes and shaking her head as Jane burst into laughter.

Chapter Seven

Jane took her place in the third pew from the front, joining Alice, who had gone ahead while she visited with a friend. It amused her that they sat in the same seat every Sunday and had since they were schoolgirls listening to their father preach. Perhaps they should vary their routine and experience the service from a back pew or a middle pew.

Jane hadn't seen Rev. Thompson since he returned from his job interview. Would he give any clue regarding his intentions in the sermon? Or would he make an announcement to the congregation? She could hardly wait to hear what he had to say.

He began his sermon by reading the parable of the lost sheep. His voice was strong as he concluded: "'I tell you that in the same way there will be more rejoicing in heaven over one sinner who repents than over ninety-nine righteous persons who do not need to repent'" (Luke 15:7).

Her father had especially liked that verse. One of Jane's early memories of his sermons was a vivid description of hunting for the lost sheep. For weeks afterward, she longed to have a lamb of her own, imagining that she would take such good care of it that it would never get lost. Her father tried to explain that it wasn't practical to keep a sheep in town. Her first cat had been a surprise from him to compensate for the lamb she couldn't have. Given her lifelong fondness for cats, she could only admire her father's wise gift.

The sermon brought back memories and gave her food for thought, but it didn't seem to have anything to do with the decision the pastor was facing. When he made the announcements for the week, they didn't contain any indication that he was thinking about leaving Grace Chapel. She allowed herself to hope that he had changed his mind, but perhaps he was only waiting until his plans were finalized.

After church, Alice left with Vera and Fred for Sunday dinner at a new restaurant in Lancaster that they'd been wanting to try. Their meal was delightful, and Vera and Alice had a chance to discuss their upcoming trip and, in particular, challenges that might be presented by young Chad.

Louise lingered at church, visiting with friends about plans the choir had to perform at another church. Jane went home alone to prepare a midday meal for the two of them. She planned to make a quiche using a homemade crust readied days ahead and stored in the freezer. She often made a breakfast quiche for the inn's guests, so it seemed practical to create one as a luncheon entrée.

By the time Louise got home, the noon meal was in the oven. Jane had added cooked chopped spinach, minced onions and thin slivers of mushrooms to the creamy quiche mixture. She first put a generous amount of grated Swiss cheese on the crust, then poured the rest of the ingredients over it. As a side dish, she cut up fresh pineapple and combined the chunks with seedless red grapes in glass sherbet cups. Her sister would say that she'd worked too hard for just the two of them, but cooking distracted her from fretting over other matters.

If Rev. Thompson left, she would miss him as a friend and mentor, and he would be extremely difficult for Grace Chapel to replace. Ministers seemed to be in short supply, and a small town like Acorn Hill was at a disadvantage in trying to attract a dedicated person to lead the congregation. Small-town life didn't appeal to everyone. She and her sisters loved the quiet friendliness and the slower pace of life, but it wasn't necessarily a selling point for others.

While Louise was changing out of the pale blue suit and lacy blouse she'd worn to church, Jane set the table in the kitchen for the two of them. When only family was eating, they preferred the cheery, casual atmosphere over the formal aura of the dining room. Jane loved the classic black-and-white checkerboard pattern of the floor tiles, the warm, rusty-red cupboards and the butcher-block countertops.

She hadn't had a chance for a long talk with her older sister for several days, given that both of them seemed to be constantly busy. She wondered if Louise's friends at church knew anything about their minister's plans. It was an honor to be taken into his confidence but, in this instance, his secret had become a personal heartache.

"I hope you haven't gone to a lot of trouble for the two of us," Louise said. "I really don't have much appetite today."

"Have you heard more about Kenneth?"

"No, not a word. I can understand his silence, though. He wouldn't want to alarm the congregation if there's any chance he won't leave."

"Then we can take it as a good sign that he hasn't said anything." Jane tried to sound more optimistic.

"Well, perhaps. I'm sure that whatever he decides, he'll try to follow God's plan for him."

Jane was afraid that he would cease using the talents that made him an exceptional minister. Maybe a new job would reenergize his commitment to the Lord, but the cost could be high. Grace Chapel would lose a dedicated minister, and he would lose much of the personal contact that provided him with friendships and made him an outstanding spiritual leader.

She served the quiche, giving them both small portions to start with.

"I had quite a visit with Sarah Lister," she said after Louise had led them in a blessing.

"She's a sweet girl—well meaning but a little flighty, I'm afraid. I feel bad that I involved you."

"I don't mind. It will be fun to make plum pudding. Sarah is going to shop for the ingredients, and we'll mix it up here. I don't see what can go wrong. I'll be here to supervise, and I'll take charge of steaming the puddings."

"Sarah seems to have a genius for turning things upside down. Nine Lives looked as if it had been hit by a tornado after she decided to dust the books," Louise said in a warning tone.

"She did take a fresh approach to that job, but it's something I might have done if I wanted to dust and reorganize Father's library."

"You don't have customers coming in and wanting to buy books here at home."

"Ah, I see the problem. But don't worry. I'll supervise her. We shouldn't have any trouble following a recipe together."

"She also has a tendency to wander off, especially when a certain young man is in the vicinity."

Jane shrugged and smiled.

The phone rang, and Jane left the table to answer it.

"Jane, this is Kenneth. I wonder if tomorrow would be a good time to get started on the rocker."

"Yes, of course. I'll be free to help any time you like. We don't have a single guest this evening, so I won't have to prepare a big breakfast. That doesn't happen very often."

"Wonderful. I'll need your expertise. I bought some paint stripper at the hardware store. Fred recommends it highly, so maybe we can make quick work of it. Also I have a supply of gloves, drop cloths, brushes and just about everything he said was necessary. The only thing I don't have is a supply of rags."

"No problem. I have plenty," Jane assured him.

They set a time that would be good for both. Then she hung up and returned to the table deep in thought.

"We're going to work on the chair tomorrow," she said unnecessarily. "I didn't want to quiz him on his plans, but I really hope he brings up the subject himself while we're working."

"It seems likely that he will. He's a very thoughtful man, and he must know you're concerned about his future," Louise assured her.

Later in the day, Jane turned her thoughts away from the pastor's decision. She needed to think about the job of refinishing his rocker. In order to frame her own art as inexpensively as possible, she'd often renovated picture frames bought at tag sales, sometimes stripping off old paint or varnish. She wasn't sure about the best way to approach this larger project, but fortunately she knew where to find help. Rev. Thompson was knowledgeable about restoring furniture, but she wanted to review her own education in the same area.

Her father had liked to renovate damaged and discarded furniture. When he could spare the time from his busy ministry and the responsibility of raising three girls on his own, he took particular pleasure in refinishing distressed pieces. Maybe it was a reflection of his love for the lesson behind the lost-sheep story. Just as he refused to abandon those who had strayed from the Lord, he didn't like to give up on furniture that had seen better days. He approached each piece with the eye of a historian, wondering about the people who had owned it and the skilled workmen who had made it. He could take a damaged tabletop or a chest with warped veneer and restore it to its original beauty. Although he'd been called to a profession that provided welcome challenges to his emotions and intelligence, he was never more content than when he was working with his hands.

She smiled as she remembered how, while still in elementary school, she'd helped him glue down the loose veneer on a console table that he refinished and later gave to Ethel as a gift from both of them. In fact, some of her happiest memories involved helping him restore the furniture he acquired.

Once his enthusiasm for finding and fixing old things became well known to the congregation, it wasn't at all unusual to wake up in the morning to find a battered castoff on the front porch. In later years, when he had less time and energy for refinishing projects, orphaned furniture tended to collect in the attic. Jane had cleaned out some of the more hopeless pieces and, someday, when time allowed, she would do something with the steamer trunk with the corroded lock, and other assorted objects too good to throw away.

Meanwhile, she wanted to be as helpful as possible to Rev. Thompson, and she knew just where to get good advice. She went to the inn's library and searched the shelves for the book her father always consulted, *The Furniture Doctor*. After several minutes of looking, she found the copy tucked away on a bottom shelf. The cover was tattered, and several stains attested to the time it had spent in the shed while he consulted it.

Making herself comfortable in one of the two russet-colored chairs chosen to complement the library's mossy green wallpaper and mahogany bookshelves, she started to flip through it.

Although she only intended to skim the pertinent parts, she soon found herself reading page after page and smiling while she did. Besides all the how-to advice, the author included lots of Yankee humor, sometimes making her laugh aloud. She didn't believe she had ever read the sections in the back of the book on furniture styles and tools, so she looked through everything the author had to offer.

An hour passed so quickly she could hardly believe it. She felt energized at the prospect of doing some refinishing projects of her own after she helped Rev. Thompson with the chair. Jane regretted not seeing more of her father in his later years. Today she felt closer to him than she had in quite a while. Reading the book that he'd frequently consulted, and remembering the times she'd helped with his projects reminded her of many nurturing hours spent with him.

∞

Jane got up even earlier than usual on Monday morning. Although she didn't have guest breakfasts to prepare, she didn't want Alice to leave on the school trip without a good meal.

"You really don't have to cook for me," her sister protested. "This was a rare chance for you to sleep late."

"I woke up early anyway. Would you like some mushrooms and green peppers in your scrambled eggs?"

"No, thank you. One egg and a piece of wheat toast will be fine. I have to admit that I'm too keyed up to eat much. I hope I'm up to keeping track of five boys."

"You will be," Jane assured her, placing a glass of freshly squeezed orange juice in front of her. "Vera has everything organized. What could possibly go wrong?"

"I could lose one." Alice smiled wanly.

"Not likely. Just enjoy yourself. Mark is giving a tour of the zoo, isn't he? That will be fun for you."

"Yes. He was kind enough to arrange something special for the class, and I look forward to seeing him."

Jane served up the egg and toast, then sat opposite her sister with a cup of orange-spice tea.

"Kenneth is coming around nine to start work on the chair. I hope he brings up the subject of whether he'll leave Grace Chapel."

"I've been praying about it. I don't want to be selfish in wanting to keep him here if the Lord has other plans for him, but he would be sorely missed."

"That he would."

Alice set off on her big adventure as a chaperone, armed with sunscreen, bottled water, and enough of Jane's home-made trail mix loaded with granola, raisins, coconut and chocolate chips to keep hunger at bay for a dozen boys.

"Have fun!" Jane called after her sister. "Maybe Vera will let you chaperone every year."

"Bite your tongue! This is more nerve-racking than emergency surgery. At least when I assist a doctor, I know the procedures. I've no idea what to expect from five excited fifth-graders."

"You can handle them. Have a good time!"

With Alice gone and Louise not downstairs yet, Jane was at loose ends. She was too focused on the project with the chair to apply herself to anything else, so she went out to the shed, taking along a big stack of old rags.

The hideous purple paint looked even worse in the light of morning, but on impulse she sat in the chair once again. It was surprisingly comfortable, owing in no small part to the padded leather seat. They would have to be exceedingly careful not to get any stripper on it. That notion led to an idea for protecting it.

She measured the leather square, then returned to the house and found an old throw rug she'd been meaning to discard. She cut and shaped it to the size of the seat with a sharp knife that she used to mat pictures before framing. It was easy to cover the resulting square of thick fabric with plastic from a new trash bag. When she was satisfied with the protective pad, she took it back to the shed and taped it over the leather seat with masking tape. If a sliver of paint remained around the seat, it would be easy enough to remove with steel wool. Rev. Thompson came to the door of the shed just as she was finishing the job.

She looked up, expecting to see the conservatively dressed minister and laughed out loud.

"Where did you get those overalls?" she gasped.

He was wearing a pair of farmer's overalls that were large enough for two men his size, but the legs barely came to the tops of his white sports socks. Under it he wore a purple plaid flannel shirt that had been laundered so much it came close to matching the color of the rocker.

"Pretty bizarre, aren't they?" he said with a grin. "A parishioner gave me these overalls. The shirt too."

He stuck his hands in the pockets of the overalls, then batted his eyes and pursed his lips like a clown's.

She couldn't help giggling. "Why?" she asked.

"I went to a guild meeting to give the opening prayer and happened to mention that I was planning to refinish a rocker, but my wardrobe didn't include any paint-stripping clothes. The next day a kind lady came by the church office with this costume. I didn't ask where she got it. Sometimes you have to accept a gift at face value. At least it will save me from ruining a pair of trousers."

Jane looked down at her rather seedy jeans and the old long-sleeved cotton shirt that she kept for painting. They both bore traces of other projects.

"I see you've covered the leather seat. Good job." He put a large plastic sack from the hardware store on the work bench and started taking things from it.

"Let's see what Fred recommended," she said, starting to read the directions on a can of stripper.

"He said one coat should be enough since we only have one layer of paint to remove."

"Fred's never steered me wrong. Good, you bought some cheap throw-away brushes to put it on. I always try to use one that's beyond its useful life. I don't mind cleaning them, but I hesitate to reuse a brush for something else after it's been saturated with stripper."

She made sure the single window of the shed was open

as far as it would go and propped the door open with the wheelbarrow she used for gardening. As a final precaution, she turned on a small portable fan to keep the air circulating, an absolute must when working with noxious chemicals. They both donned heavy rubber gloves, then, by unspoken agreement, she began spreading the thick mixture around the seat and over the arms, while Kenneth turned his attention to the back of the chair. The task went fast with both of them working in silent concentration.

"Now, if Fred is right," Rev. Thompson said when all the exposed areas were covered with stripper, "we'll be able to lift off the paint layer with a putty knife after it sits awhile."

"It sounds easy, doesn't it?"

Removing paint was never quite as easy as the directions on the stripper container made it sound. No doubt stubborn spots would require separate applications and possibly the use of steel wool. Once they saw what was under the paint, the pastor would have to decide whether to bleach or stain the wood. Jane's instinct was to retain the original color whenever possible, but he might have another idea. The thought occurred to her that he might have to hurry the job if he planned to move, but she didn't want to mention it.

"We have a little wait. Would you like to come in for coffee or tea?" she asked.

"With pleasure."

They hadn't talked about anything but the job at hand. Would he say anything about his job interview over coffee? Jane could only wonder.

She made coffee using a hazelnut blend from the gourmet coffee shop in Potterston, a brew that often brought compliments from the inn's guests. Because she'd expected him to accept an invitation for coffee, she'd made a pan of molasses cookies. She knew from church suppers that he liked spicy foods. Her cookies were extra spicy, a perfect mid-morning treat.

"Well, that went well," he said when they'd settled down at the table. "You worked with the paint stripper so easily that I'm guessing you have a lot of experience."

"I used to help my father, and, of course, I've done a lot of frames for my artwork."

"Good cookie," he said, absentmindedly taking a bite and then stirring half-and-half into the dark, steaming coffee. "You're probably wondering how my interview went last week."

"Well, I have been concerned."

"The truth is, I haven't made my decision yet."

"Does that mean you were offered the job?"

"Yes."

"It would be a very different job from the excellent work you've been doing." She tried not to sound critical, but she was greatly saddened by the thought of his departure.

"There are many ways of serving the Lord." He didn't make it sound like a reprimand.

"Yes, of course." She wanted to say something about using God-given talents in the best way possible but didn't feel that it was her place to lecture a minister.

"I have one week to make a decision. I promised to let them know next Monday."

"Which way are you leaning?"

He looked unhappy, but he only shook his head.

"The congregation would really miss you," she said softly.

"Only for a short while. The chapel might call a younger minister, one with new ideas and more energy."

"Ministers like that are hard to find. So are those who care as much about others as you do."

"You're giving me more credit than I deserve. From everything I've learned since coming here, your father gave Grace Chapel a depth of spiritual leadership and Christian example that I can't begin to approach."

"You're selling yourself short, Kenneth. If Father were

still with us, he would wholeheartedly approve of your ministry."

He was still stirring his coffee, staring at the mocha brown liquid in the cup instead of looking up at her. She realized how hard this decision was for him, but her heart still cried out for him to stay. What could she say or do to convince him that his calling at Grace Chapel was bearing fruit, that he was treasured for reaching out to people in need every day?

"You're a good friend, Jane. You and your sisters have supported my ministry from the first day. You don't know how much that means. Even though I work with people all the time, the job can still be a lonely one."

"Kenneth, that sounds like a good-bye speech."

"No, I really haven't made my decision yet."

He sipped his coffee, seemingly unwilling to say more about changing jobs. Jane filled the time by telling him about Alice's trip to Philadelphia and Louise's challenge at the bookstore, but her heart wasn't in it.

After a while, he looked at the clock on the kitchen wall.

"Maybe we should check on the chair," he said.

"Yes, the stripper's had time to work."

She followed him out to the shed, but the fun had gone out of the project.

Chapter Eight

Alice arrived at the elementary school early on Monday morning, but a crowd had already gathered outside the school bus that would take Vera's fifth-grade class to Philadelphia. Alice guessed that many children had insisted on being there ahead of time in order not to miss the departure. Thinking back to her own childhood, she knew that both she and Louise had always been among the first to arrive for important events.

She spotted two of her boys, Andrew and Alex, huddled at the back of the group, and Erik was just being dropped off by his father in a white sedan. There was still plenty of time for the other two, Matt and Chad, to get there.

"Good morning, Alice," Vera said, walking up to her. "Are you ready to have fun?"

"As ready as I'll ever be." She smiled, hoping she didn't look as nervous as she felt.

"You'll be in charge of a nice group of boys. Erik is unusually responsible for his age, and Andrew is a born organizer. He dots every I and crosses every T. I did want to have another word with you about Chad." She drew Alice off to the side for privacy.

"Is there a problem?"

"No, I'm sure he'll behave for you, but he is going through a bad patch. His parents have separated, and he's taking it hard. As I understand it, his father has left the family, and his older brother is away at college. His mother is having a hard time dealing with the prospect of a divorce. Chad's reaction has been to withdraw. He's alienated his friends and fallen off badly in his schoolwork."

"That's so sad," Alice said.

"I don't think he'll misbehave. He hasn't been acting up in class, and he's not rowdy or defiant. I just want you to know that if he seems surly or unhappy, it's not because of anything you may or may not have done."

"Thanks, I'm glad to know that."

"Don't get on the bus yet, girls," Vera called out, distracted by a pair who were headed for the open door of the vehicle. "You should meet the other chaperones, Alice. Come on, I'll introduce you to my student teacher. She's one of the best I've ever had."

She led Alice over to the group of adults who had congregated off to the side of the children.

"Alice, this is Caitlin Abbot. She's been so helpful this semester that I'll be sorry to see her graduate. Caitlin, this is my dear friend, Alice Howard. She agreed to help when I couldn't get our quota of chaperones. I told the kids to call her Miss Alice."

"It's nice to meet you, Caitlin."

"Nice to meet you." The young woman smiled.

"Thanks again for hooking us up with Dr. Graves at the zoo," Vera said as she steered Alice toward the other chaperones. "It will be the highlight of the trip. The kids in my class love animals."

"Mr. Nichols, Mrs. Nichols, this is Alice Howard," Vera said, stopping in front of a handsome couple. "Alice doesn't have a child in school, but she's helping us out." She turned to Alice. "The Nichols have twin girls."

"We're Dave and Beth," the mother said. "My husband is taking a day off work to chaperone."

"It's the least I can do," the stocky, muscular man said. "Our girls are double trouble."

"Not at all," Vera said, "but we're certainly glad to have both of you along. I should explain one thing. The kids have a buddy system. Every child is supposed to stick with a partner. You only need to worry about the children in your assigned group."

Out of the corner of her eye, Alice saw another of her boys, Matt, arrive wearing a bright orange jacket and carrying a black backpack with fluorescent-green and yellow trim. At least he would be easy to see in a crowd. He joined the three boys who were there ahead of him, and the four of them talked together while they waited. Not having met Chad, Alice didn't know whether he had arrived.

The final chaperone was Bonnie Green, a cousin of Rose Bellwood, the mother of a farm family Alice had known for some time. She hadn't been introduced to Bonnie before this, but her broad, friendly face was familiar. Perhaps they'd been at the same event sometime.

"It's time to take a count," Vera announced to everyone within hearing. "The children have numbers to sound off, so we can do it quickly. Leaving someone behind is not an option." This she said loudly, getting the attention of everyone waiting to board the bus.

"Okay, start counting."

"One," a boy at the back of the group shouted energetically.

After a pause following seventeen, the count got to twenty-seven, with four of Alice's five boys calling out their numbers.

"Where's eighteen?" Vera asked, consulting a list she'd been carrying in her large striped canvas bag. "Chad? If you're here, call out your number."

Everyone was still, and it became obvious that Chad wasn't among them.

"I'll give him a call on my cell phone," Vera said.

Alice didn't hear the conversation, but she did see Vera's face. She didn't look happy.

"His mother sent him off on foot about half an hour ago," Vera said with a worried expression. "I would hate to leave him behind, but we're on a tight schedule. I tried to impress on the children how important it is to be on time. I do wish that she'd brought him here herself. As far as I know, she has a car. If not, I'm sure another parent would have been happy to pick him up."

"What will you do if he doesn't come?" Alice asked. "If you know where he lives, maybe I can walk that way and see if he's coming."

"That's nice of you, but there isn't even time for that. There are several different streets he could have taken. If he left half an hour ago, something is wrong."

"Is it possible he doesn't want to go?" Alice felt as worried as Vera looked.

Suddenly, several voices cried out at once.

"There's Chad."

"If he walked any slower, he wouldn't be moving," a boy said.

"I knew that loser would be late," another youngster said, pointing at a figure still some distance away.

Vera hurried off to start loading the bus, and Alice let out a sigh of concern. Was Chad's tardiness a sign of what the day would bring?

"Dear Lord," she said under her breath, "please help us on this journey."

The children were filing onto the bus in an orderly manner, Vera and the student teacher standing on either side of the door to check their names off a list.

"Remember, whatever seat you choose, you're to sit in it for the whole trip," Vera said.

The chaperones hung back, waiting until the children were seated before they, too, boarded the bus. Not surprisingly, the front seats had been left vacant for them. In fairly short order, everyone but she and Vera was on the bus. Chad was still a block away and showing no signs of hurrying.

He was wearing a hooded maroon sweatshirt several sizes too large, tan cargo pants with pockets in the legs and a green baseball cap worn backward. The brown hair hanging over his forehead was uncombed, and his face was thin with a small mouth and a pug nose. Alice could see rebellion in the slouch of his shoulders and the slow swagger in his stride.

"Please do hurry, Chad," Vera said when he was within hearing. "We're ready to leave."

If her request persuaded him to walk any faster, Alice couldn't detect it. But he finally climbed up the bus steps, and she and Vera followed.

"Where am I supposed to sit?" he asked belligerently, looking down the aisle of the crowded interior.

"The only seat left is here in front," Vera said, indicating the double seat across from the one she and her student teacher would occupy in order to be directly behind the bus driver.

Alice understood that the teacher and her helper had to sit there to be able to confer with the patiently smiling driver. His looks were undistinguished, but his wrinkles all seemed to be smile lines. Vera had introduced him to the group as Mr. Boswell.

Standing until Chad reluctantly flopped down in the seat by the window, Vera gave Alice an apologetic shrug. "You'll be sitting next to Miss Alice, Chad. She kindly volunteered to be one of our chaperones. That will be your seat for the whole trip."

"I don't want to sit in front."

"When you're late, you don't have a choice. Remember

your group of buddies. You're to stay with them whenever we get off the bus."

He slumped down in the seat and crossed his arms over his chest, radiating dissatisfaction but not saying anything. Alice sat beside him and tried to decide whether to try talking to him. She could understand that a boy his age would prefer to sit with another classmate, but it seemed that neither of them had a choice. She decided to give him time to accept his situation. Maybe he was a person who woke up out of sorts in the morning and got over his grumpiness as the day progressed. She hoped that was the case.

The children were buzzing with anticipation as the bus left town. Alice found their muted conversations oddly soothing and felt her eyelids drooping. She had to shake her head and focus on staying awake. It wouldn't do for one of the chaperones to fall asleep, perhaps to snore.

The first part of the ride was a bit monotonous for her. The bus headed toward Potterston, the same route she took to work at the hospital. She found her head nodding in spite of her determination to stay alert.

Chad had had enough time to sulk. She needed to talk to stay awake, and the trip would be much more pleasant for both of them if she could find some common ground between them.

"What part of the trip do you think you'll enjoy most, Chad?"

It was a typical adult-to-child question, she immediately realized, but she was at a loss to think of a better conversation starter.

"None."

"The zoo trip should be fun," she said.

"Bunch of dumb animals."

"Was this trip optional—did you have to come?"

"I know what *optional* means. My mother wouldn't let

me stay home. If I went to school today, I'd have to stay in the fourth-grade room all day."

"Yes, I can see where you wouldn't enjoy that," Alice said sympathetically.

She was used to handling sick children. What she had to remember was that this boy was sick at heart over his parents' separation. He needed patience and understanding as much as a child who came to the emergency room injured or ill.

"When my family went on trips, my sisters and I used to play the alphabet game. It helped pass the time. What you do is find something outside the bus that begins with the letter *A*, then the next person has to find something that begins with *B*. Would you like to play?"

He didn't answer, so she took it as agreement.

"I'll go first. There's an automobile coming toward us. That will be my *A*. Your turn is *B*."

They passed a bush, a branch, a bicycle and a barn. The game came back to her quickly, but she seemed to be playing alone.

Just when she thought Chad wasn't interested, he said, "Baboon."

"Yes, I imagine we'll see some at the zoo."

"That's my *B*. Baboon."

"I'm afraid I don't see it."

"Up there, that cloud looks like a baboon."

She bent a bit, trying to see Chad's baboon in the sky, but the clouds seemed too thin and scattered. Either he had an especially active imagination or he was putting her on. She guessed the latter.

"All right, if you see it, I'll count it. Now my letter is *C*, and you've already given me an answer. Cloud. You need to find *D*."

A half hour later, Chad still hadn't called out the name of an object that began with *D*. Alice conceded that her idea to draw him out hadn't worked but hoped Chad would be in a happier frame of mind when they got to Philadelphia. He would see the sights, and he might enjoy himself in spite of his poor start.

"We're nearly there," Mr. Boswell announced after what seemed to Alice like a long ride. "If we don't get delayed by road construction problems, we'll get to the Independence National Historical Park in fifteen or twenty minutes."

Scattered cheers broke out among the children, and Alice felt like joining them. Philadelphia was just over an hour from Acorn Hill, but riding with her silent seatmate made it seem longer.

The bus did get tied up in traffic delays several times before reaching an area in the heart of the old city that had been set aside as a national park because of its historical importance. Vera used the time to review with the students what they had learned about their nation's struggle for independence. Alice found herself listening with interest, admiring the way Vera put things on the children's level without talking down to them.

There was excitement in the air when Mr. Boswell parked the bus and everyone exited. Caitlin checked to see that everyone was following the buddy system, while Vera made sure no one was left behind. They worked so efficiently that Alice wondered whether Vera and her student teacher could have handled the trip without additional chaperones.

Their first destination was Independence Visitor Center, where Vera would pick up the tickets reserved ahead of time for the Independence Hall tour. The children were allowed to view exhibits and use restrooms, and Alice got her first hint of what was involved in being a chaperone. Her five boys started to scatter, but she reined them in and cautioned them to stay together. When the boys went into a men's lavatory, she could only hope all five would emerge again. Several minutes later, four came out.

"Erik, Matt, Alex, Andrew." she said their names aloud to get their attention. "Where's Chad?"

They gave her a blank look.

"Erik, you and Matt are supposed to stay with Chad."

"I thought he was with us," Matt said.

"I'll go check," Erik offered, disappearing into the restroom.

She waited a minute or so, but neither boy returned. Much to her relief, Dave Nichols, the father of the twins, approached them.

"I'm short one boy," she explained to him. "The boy I sent to look for him hasn't come out either. Would you mind checking on them? Their names are Chad and Erik."

Mr. Nichols returned in a minute or so, escorting the two boys.

"We had a little game of hide-and-seek going in there," he explained.

"It wasn't my fault," Erik protested vehemently. "I don't know why I have to babysit Chad."

"I'm not a baby," Chad said angrily. "I didn't ask to hang out with you."

"That's enough, guys!" Mr. Nichols said in a commanding voice that quieted them. "It's time to meet our group."

Alice thanked him, but she felt even more inadequate about riding herd on her boys. She hoped they would stick together for the rest of the trip, but she already had regrets about coming.

The children were milling around, talking, giggling and obviously enjoying themselves. Alice was wondering how Vera would get their attention just a moment before her friend raised her arms above her head. To Alice's surprise, the group quieted almost immediately.

"Good, you remembered our signal," Vera said. "We have time to see the Liberty Bell before our tour of Independence Hall. Just to be sure everyone is here, let's sound off."

The fifth graders called out their numbers with no delay. Alice was impressed with how well her friend had organized the trip. No doubt she was worrying for nothing. Now that all her boys were out in the open where she could keep an eye on them, there was no way she would let them scatter.

After a minor bit of jostling for position, the whole group moved off toward the special structure that housed the Liberty Bell. When they got there, they had to wait their turn to pass through a security check for visitors.

"What's the most important thing you know about the Liberty Bell?" Vera asked, turning to face the students.

"It's cracked," a voice called out.

"Yes, I'm sure we'll hear more about that from the tour guide," she said. "The bell rang for a very important event. Who remembers what it was?"

"To call people to hear the Declaration of Independence," Andrew said.

"The first Fourth of July in 1776," Alex added.

Alice felt a flash of pride that her boys had answered the question.

"Good," Vera said. "It was actually a few days later, on July 8, that the bell rang for the first public reading, but the Liberty Bell will always be associated with freedom."

As they gradually moved forward, it didn't take Alice long to realize that her boys were more interested in the security check than in the bell. They were delighted when Mr. Nichols had to take off his shoes because there were steel plates in the soles.

"Just like in the movies," Chad said with satisfaction, speaking for the first time since they'd started walking to the bell.

"My dad had to take off his shoes and his jacket when he flew to Los Angeles," Andrew said.

"Yeah, I'll bet they thought he was dangerous," Erik teased.

The boys exchanged good-natured barbs, but as soon as Andrew mentioned his father, Chad became silent again, turning away from the others.

This time Alice kept a careful watch on him, grateful when they were all in the confines of the building. She was pretty sure the other four would stay with the group, so she decided to keep her attention riveted on the unpredictable Chad.

When the students pressed ahead for a better view of the bell, Vera slipped up to Alice.

"Everything seems to be going well so far," she said softly. "Any problem with Chad?"

"He hid in the restroom, but Dave Nichols fetched him for me. I'll keep a close eye on him for the rest of the day."

"I think he'll be all right. He's a bright boy, and he's shown some interest in history. I hope he'll enjoy what he's seeing and won't cause problems. If you have any trouble, let me know."

"Let's hope I won't need to." Alice smiled to reassure her friend.

The guide was a pleasant, round-faced young man who smiled frequently and seemed to have infinite patience with his young audience. He explained that the Liberty Bell had moved to this special structure in 2003 so it could be better seen and protected.

"How did it crack?" a young voice called out.

"Ah, we'll get to that soon. First, can you read what's written on the bell?" The group peered at the writing, but he read it before anyone could answer.

"By Order of the Assembly of the Province of Pensylvania for the State House in Philada."

"It's not spelled right," Erik pointed out.

"You're absolutely right. By today's standards, both *Pennsylvania* and *Philadelphia* are spelled wrong. In those days, people pretty much decided for themselves how to spell different words. If you go to the second floor of Independence

Hall, you'll see a map that spells *Pennsylvania* the same way as on the bell. And instead of calling the ocean the Atlantic, the mapmaker named it the Western Ocean."

"He's lucky he didn't have Mrs. Humbert for a spelling teacher," an unidentified voice called out, followed by a burst of laughter.

"There's more writing." The guide pointed at the bell behind its protective casing. "Proclaim Liberty throughout all the land unto all the inhabitants thereof."

The words were familiar to Alice, but she didn't immediately realize how familiar.

"It's a quote from the Bible, Leviticus 25:10," the guide said. "Freedom was a new and exciting idea in 1776. The Pennsylvania Assembly—that was their legislature—quoted the Bible on the bell for the belfry of their state house, what we now call Independence Hall."

The children were quiet now, trying to absorb everything the charismatic guide told them.

"You know how artists like to sign the pictures they paint, don't you?" he asked.

Several young people murmured agreement.

"Well, we have a signature on the bell too. 'Pass and Stow/Philada/MDCCLIII.' Now we'll come to the part about the crack."

He took a breath and continued enthusiastically. "The original idea was to commission a bell to mark the fiftieth anniversary of William Penn's 1701 Charter of Privileges for the colony of Pennsylvania. This was an important document that gave religious freedom to the people of the colony and allowed them to participate in enacting laws. They wanted the bell to be special, so they ordered it from London. But when it was installed and they rang it, something was wrong. The bell cracked. What do you think they did then?"

"Tried to patch it?" Erik asked.

"No, they gave it to a Philadelphia foundry to break into pieces and melt it down. John Pass and John Stow were the men who cast the second bell using the metal from the original one. They added copper to make it stronger and less brittle, but that's not the end of the story."

"When did it crack again?" another curious voice asked.

"It took a long time. The copper they added made it sound different. Some said they put in too much. No one liked the tone of the new bell. They took it down, and Pass and Stow melted it to cast it another time. Remember, this bell weighed 2,080 pounds and had to be raised to the top of what we now call Independence Hall. And guess what?"

"It cracked?" Andrew asked.

"No, not yet, but people still didn't like the way it sounded. They ordered another bell from England, but when it came, it didn't sound any better. The second bell made by Pass and Stow stayed in the steeple, and here it is today."

"It didn't sound right, and it cracked. It's not much of a bell," a young skeptic said.

"It was some time before it cracked again, but no one is quite sure exactly when. The damage became serious when it rang for George Washington's birthday in 1846. Before then it tolled for many important events. Remember, there were no radios or televisions in those days. The people needed a way of letting everyone know when something significant was happening. The bell could be heard for long distances in the city."

The guide said the bell rang when Ben Franklin was leaving for England to take colonial grievances to the English government's attention, and again for the Battle of Lexington and Concord.

He was a skilled lecturer, but he also knew when to stop. His young audience started to fidget and lose interest in the list of historical events, so he recaptured their interest with a question.

"Do you know what the British did with the bells they found when they occupied the colonies?"

This time there was no response.

"They melted all they could find to make cannons. The people of Philadelphia didn't want their bells used against them, so they took them all down and hid them. They saved the Liberty Bell in 1777 by transporting it to Allentown and hiding it under the floorboards of a church there."

The mention of cannons stimulated the interest of several boys in the group, and the guide answered questions until Vera signaled that it was time to leave. They weren't the only school group visiting the historical sites, and it was important that they be on time for their tour of Independence Hall.

Alice found her boys bunched together in the midst of the group and counted five heads including Chad's, which was easy to spot with his backward baseball cap. They'd all been attentive while the guide talked about the Liberty Bell. Would their interest last all day?

She remembered that when the bell rang in 1776, it was only the beginning of the struggle.

Chapter  Nine

The Acorn Hill fifth graders had a short wait outside Independence Hall before beginning their tour. The air held the balmy promise of spring, but most of the students still wore their colorful jackets or hooded sweatshirts.

Alice stayed close to her five boys, although she felt like an invisible woman. They were totally absorbed in a conversation about video games, but she knew absolutely nothing about such games or about using the computer for recreation. She listened and tried to learn. Actually, only four of them were talking. Chad stood off to the side and didn't join in their discussion. She wasn't sure whether he isolated himself or the others excluded him.

Although she was fond of children, she didn't know enough about young boys to understand them well. The girls in her ANGELs group often shared their thoughts with her, and she felt blessed to have their confidence. Unfortunately, she was a stranger to the fifth-grade boys, and they were too busy with each other for her to get to know them better.

She very much wished that there was a way to help Chad gain status with his peers and become an accepted part of the group, but she didn't know how to do it. She thought of speaking to Vera, but her friend was too busy supervising the whole excursion.

The trip was certainly giving Alice a new appreciation for teachers. Vera was matter-of-fact about what she did as an educator, but it was nothing short of amazing the way she kept track of details and answered the needs of twenty-five young people. The key seemed to be planning ahead and anticipating everything that might come up. No wonder Vera spent many hours during the summer break working on the next year's lessons. People who envied teachers' long vacations had no idea how important it was for them to recharge their batteries and come up with new and innovative ways of reaching the children under their care.

Their group was allowed to enter the historic building at almost exactly the time indicated on their tickets. Alice was in awe of all that had been accomplished in the lovely Georgian building that once served as colonial Pennsylvania's seat of government. She listened intently to everything the Department of the Interior guide—a uniformed young woman who radiated friendliness— had to say. Instead of just lecturing, the guide caught the children's attention by asking questions they could answer.

"What's the most important thing that ever happened around here?" she asked.

"They rang the Liberty Bell," a young voice called out.

"They certainly did, but do you remember why?"

"To have people come hear the Declaration of Independence," Andrew said, by now sounding like an expert on the bell.

"Very good." She gave him a high-voltage smile, and Alice was proud of him. "Our founding fathers also drafted the Constitution here one hot summer in 1787. They kept all the windows closed so their discussions weren't overheard. Can you imagine how uncomfortable that must have been before air-conditioning?"

Alice moved with her group into the Assembly Room, which contained tables covered with cloths. Books and papers were arranged on them as though the legislators had just stepped out for a break.

"Look at all the candles," a voice behind her said.

"They didn't have electric lights then, dummy," Chad commented.

Chad's remark was unkind, and Alice could sense the unhappiness in the boy. She tried to tell herself that there was nothing she could do, but she'd been caring for sick children too long to ignore him.

The students seemed especially intrigued by George Washington's chair, elevated at the front of the room. It dated from the time when Philadelphia was named as the nation's capital in 1790. A couple of girls behind Alice quietly debated whether the wooden back really looked like a rising sun—the description given to the chair—until Vera signaled for them to stop talking. Most of the fifth graders seemed genuinely interested in the guide's lecture, which made the chaperones' job much easier.

"All of the furniture on display dates from the correct time period, but much of it wasn't originally used here. There's one important exception. President Washington's chair is the one he actually used," the guide explained, patiently taking questions whenever the children raised their hands.

Alice enjoyed all the displays, especially the inkwell used in the signing of the Declaration of Independence and the Constitution.

The children showed that they had been listening to the guide at the Liberty Bell. When the new guide pointed out an antique map on display, several were quick to point out words misspelled in the same way as those on the bell.

By the end of the tour, Alice was proud of the group's good behavior and worthwhile questions. While they filed back outside, she heard snatches of conversation that confirmed the children's interest in what they had seen.

She got ahead of her group of boys and looked back to see Erik leading the others toward the designated meeting place, where the two teachers were waiting for them with arms upraised. Alice stopped for a moment to take a quick count. Matt was beside Erik, while Alex and Andrew were deep in conversation behind them.

"One, two, three, four," she said out loud, trying to spot Chad among the stragglers.

He was nowhere to be seen.

"Where's Chad?" she asked, hurrying back to the other four.

They all looked around them, but it was obvious that, once again, Chad had slipped away.

Alice wanted to scold his classmates for losing him, but it wasn't really their fault that he kept wandering off.

"Tell Mrs. Humbert that I'm going to look for him," she told Erik.

She couldn't go back inside Independence Hall now that she'd exited. Fortunately the same guide was still in front of the building, and Alice quickly explained that one of their boys was missing and possibly still inside the building.

Vera, looking irritated, hurried over to join her.

"Chad again! This disappearing act has got to stop."

"I'm terribly sorry," Alice apologized. "I'm really trying to keep track of him."

"It's not at all your fault. He's doing this deliberately, and he knows better. I really would like to call both his parents in for a conference."

Vera went back to tell the other chaperones to go on without them, then returned to Alice as the main group headed toward the restaurant where their lunch would be waiting. After a few more anxious moments, the guide returned without Chad by her side.

"This is a new one for me," the young woman said, "but

I'm certain he isn't inside. Maybe he slipped away when the others were walking out. I can alert security if you like."

"We'll have a look around outside first," Vera said. "Thank you for your help and for a very interesting tour."

She and Alice went in opposite directions to cover the perimeter of the building. Alice felt her heart pounding with anxiety. In spite of the cozy ambiance of the historical district, Philadelphia was a large city. She didn't want to think about the possible dangers to a young boy wandering on his own. She searched for several minutes without success, then doubled back to see if Vera had found him. Much to her relief, Vera and Chad were together, walking to find her.

"I just wanted to see what was in back of the building," Chad said unconvincingly as he shuffled along beside his teacher with his eyes riveted on the ground.

"Chad, this kind of behavior has got to stop," Vera said in a sterner voice than Alice had ever heard from her. "You have two choices. You can stick with Miss Alice and your buddy group—I mean never get more than a foot from one of them—or you can stay by my side. I guarantee you won't wander off when you're with me. Which will it be?"

"My group," he mumbled.

"All right, but I want you to promise you won't pull your disappearing act again."

"I didn't notice where everybody was going. I was surprised when no one went the way I did." His story had changed, but apparently his attitude hadn't.

"Promise!" Vera firmly insisted.

"I promise." He kept his eyes on the ground.

"Now we have to hurry. Our lunches are preordered, and we mustn't be late."

They walked on either side of Chad. Alice wanted to apologize again to Vera for losing track of the boy, but this wasn't the time. She didn't like that she had to police him.

This boy was exactly what she feared when she agreed to chaperone, and she was at a loss how to reach out to him. He scarcely acknowledged her existence. Maybe her first misgivings were correct. She didn't have as much experience relating to boys as she did to girls. The boys' interests were totally foreign to her. They spoke a different language when they talked to each other. What on earth was this RuneScape computer game that they were so excited about? What could she possibly say to Chad during the rest of the day? She had to stick close to him, but she felt so awkward not knowing how to communicate with him.

They walked several blocks to a restaurant that specialized in hoagies. It had a pleasant outdoor patio with red-and-white striped umbrellas shading the tables, the perfect place to feed a large group of children. Most of the Acorn Hill group were already seated, and Alice again appreciated Vera's organizing skills. Caitlin and a pair of waitresses were distributing hefty sandwiches and beverages to the group.

"Salami and cheese," the student teacher called out, and several hands went up.

"We had the children preorder the kind of sandwich they wanted so the restaurant could have them ready when we got here," Vera explained. "Usually their customers walk past a long counter and select the bread and fillings they want, but it would be a long process with a group this size. I ordered ham and cheese with lettuce, tomato and dill pickles for you. I hope that's okay. If not, I'll trade you for my tuna salad."

"The order is fine, thank you. I'm happy to try any of Philadelphia's famous hoagies."

"Chad, there's Erik and Matt. They've saved a seat for you at their table. Sit there and don't get up without permission from Miss Alice until it's time to leave," Vera said.

He walked over to his classmates at the slowest possible pace and plopped down beside Matt. Alice couldn't hear their conversation, but Chad seemed to be avoiding the other boys' questions.

Vera invited her to sit at a round table with Caitlin and the other chaperones. Alice took a chair that allowed her to see what her group, particularly Chad, was doing. Her giant sandwich came wrapped in paper inside a plastic bag that included napkins and packets of condiments. A waitress came by and offered her a choice of coffee, tea or soda, and she gratefully opted for a glass of iced tea.

"Does anyone know why these giant sandwiches are called hoagies?" Vera asked, standing to be heard.

No one responded. Alice realized that she didn't know either.

"I've heard several different stories, but people seem to agree that the name originated right here in Philadelphia," she said. "A place near here known as Hog Island was a shipbuilding center. The men who built the ships during World War I were Italian immigrants. Who remembers when that war was fought?"

"Early in the 1900s," a girl called out.

"That's right. Shipbuilding was hard work, and the men worked long days. Naturally they got really hungry by lunchtime, and their wives made giant sandwiches with cold meat, spices, oil, tomatoes, onions and peppers, all good things that people still like. The workers named the sandwiches hoagies after Hog Island, although the spelling is different today.

"Another popular story is that an Irish worker on Hog Island saw the wonderful sandwiches an Italian brought every day. He wanted one so badly that he offered to pay if the Italian would bring an extra one for him. Everyone started calling it a Hogan because that was the name of the man who started buying them."

"My sister loves looking into the origins of different dishes," Alice said to the people at her table after Vera sat to eat her lunch. "I'll have to tell her the Hog Island story."

"I've always called this kind of sandwich a submarine," the student teacher said. "Of course, we moved here from the Midwest. Maybe it's a regional name."

"My favorite name for a huge sandwich is a Dagwood Bumstead," Alice said. "Remember the comic strip where he piled everything possible on the sandwiches he made?"

"We used to call it a hero sandwich," Vera said. "I've heard them called po'boys and Zeppelins too. Whatever you call them, this is delicious. I never thought of putting black olives on tuna."

Alice enjoyed her sandwich and the conversation with the other chaperones, but she kept an eye on Chad. Would he honor his promise to stick with his classmates? One thing was sure: She wasn't going to let him out of her sight at the zoo. The thought of searching that huge complex of animal attractions for one lost boy was too daunting to consider.

"Mr. Boswell keeps his bus nice and clean," Vera said, standing to tell the children that they would be boarding in ten minutes. "We're not going to take leftovers or sodas with us. Next stop, the Philadelphia Zoo, the first zoo established in this country."

There was some confusion, and a few children were a little boisterous. But, all in all, the fifth graders cleaned up after themselves and got on the bus with very little trouble. Vera had an instinct for being where she was needed and keeping her students calm.

Most importantly, the children counted off like clockwork. Each and every student called out a number and got on the bus. Chad took his place in the window seat beside Alice.

As the bus drove off, Alice asked him about a few of the things he'd seen, but he answered mostly in monosyllables. He wasn't rude, only distant. It made her sad that the young boy seemed to be carrying such a heavy load. Much as she wanted to say something that would cheer him, she was at a loss.

Traffic seemed to have gotten much heavier since their arrival in the city. Vera reassured the driver that they were ahead of schedule, but it was obvious that he was unhappy about the frequent stops and delays.

"If things are this snarled up on the JFK, I hate to think how long we'll be tied up on the Schuylkill," he said, referring to major roadways in the city. "I guess road construction season has started with a vengeance."

"Is there any other route to the zoo?" Vera asked, checking her wristwatch.

"I could try the Ben Franklin Parkway and see how that's moving," he said a bit dubiously.

Alice didn't know Philadelphia well, but she did have a glimmer of an idea.

"Are we going to pass anywhere near the Philadelphia Museum of Art?" she asked.

"Not if we go the way I planned," Mr. Boswell said. "But since we're barely moving, we don't have much to lose by making a detour."

"We really don't have time to visit the museum," Vera said in a soft voice that barely carried over to Alice.

"Oh, that's not what I had in mind." Alice leaned across the aisle and whispered to her.

"I think we will swing past the Museum of Art," Vera said, "if you don't mind, Mr. Boswell."

"No trouble for me," he agreed cheerfully.

Chad was absorbed in unraveling the cuff of his sweatshirt, winding the kinky thread around his finger so tightly that Alice was afraid he would cut off the circulation. On impulse, she reached over and snapped off the thread, then spoke for his ears only.

Surprisingly, he seemed interested in what she had to say. He even responded with comments of his own.

"Don't say anything until we get there," she cautioned in a low whisper.

Mr. Boswell deserved a medal for the way he maneuvered the bus through heavy noontime traffic. Alice checked her own watch, relieved that they did have plenty of time to get to the zoo. Mark Graves was taking time out of his busy schedule as head vet to give them a guided tour, and she was looking forward to it. He was a great storyteller and, no doubt, he would entertain and educate the children about many things that they ordinarily wouldn't learn on a trip to the zoo.

She looked forward to seeing Mark even though they wouldn't have any time alone. Their college relationship was ancient history, but they'd developed a warm friendship in recent years. It always boosted her spirits to know that he had, at last, accepted the Lord as his savior, and they were never at a loss for conversation in that regard.

"When will we get there?" Chad asked, the first time he had spoken to her without any prompting.

"It depends on the traffic. I shouldn't think it will take more than fifteen or twenty minutes, less if we're lucky."

"Okay."

Alice sat back and tried to relax, but the front seat gave her an unobstructed view of the road ahead and events hindering the progress of the bus. Traffic seemed as heavy or heavier than on the other route. Was she wasting time on this well-planned day? Was she overstepping her role as chaperone by suggesting a detour? Would the children be at all interested?

She caught herself fiddling with a button on her lightweight green jacket. She released it and forced herself to fold her hands sedately on her lap. It was too late to call it off. Mr. Boswell had all he could do to move forward in his lane. There was no way he would want to maneuver across heavy traffic to change lanes or find a way back to his original route. For better or worse, she was shanghaiing the fifth grade.

Soon, things began to clear up. Traffic began to part before them, and Mr. Boswell made his way to the front of the Philadelphia Museum of Art without tie-ups. Even luckier, he found a place to park the bus within easy walking distance of Alice's goal.

The children were puzzled by the unscheduled stop, but they followed Vera's directions and climbed off the bus to wait in a group on the sidewalk.

"Chad, lead the way," Alice said.

He walked with purpose toward the statue at the bottom of the museum's steps and stopped at the base.

"Tell us what it is, Chad," Alice prompted as everyone looked up at a larger-than-life bronze statue of a boxer.

"It's Rocky, the fighter from the movie. Rocky wanted to be the world champion, but no one thought he could do it. They called him a loser. Everybody said there was no way he was going to win. But he worked and worked and worked. One thing he did to train for the big fight was run up these steps. There are seventy-two of them, and at the top, he did this." Chad raised his fists in the air in triumph, the same pose as the statue's.

"A lot of people didn't want the Rocky statue on display at the art museum," Alice explained. "They said it's just a movie prop, not art. It used to stand at the top of the steps. Then it went to a sports complex. The statue eventually went into storage, but now it's back."

"Just like Rocky," Chad said. "They couldn't keep him from winning, and they couldn't keep his statue hidden. Now it's here at the bottom of the steps where he used to run."

"They brought him back because tourists love to run up the steps and raise their fists in the air at the top," Alice said.

Chad looked at Vera, and she nodded her head in approval.

Much to the other children's surprise, Chad started sprinting up the steep flight of stairs. Matt was the first to follow him, whooping with excitement as he tried to catch him. Erik followed on his heels with Andrew and Alex right behind. Some children looked toward their teacher for permission, but soon they were all racing up the seventy-two steps to the top where the art museum sat in sedate dignity.

The young student teacher and Mr. Nichols, the twins' father, were quick to start running upward themselves. Mrs. Nichols and the Bellwood cousin followed at a more sedate pace, but Vera remained standing beside Alice with a big grin on her face.

"What made you think of this?" Vera asked.

"I'm not sure. I read in the paper a while ago that the Rocky statue was being returned to the art museum, but the directors insisted it be at the bottom of the steps. Apparently, tourists came just to see Rocky. Many didn't even go inside the museum. Some critics are upset, but it is good fun, don't you think?"

"It is," Vera agreed. "And you seem to have found the one student who knows a lot about Rocky."

"I guess Chad is feeling very much the underdog in his class. Maybe this will make the trip a little more fun for him."

"Thank you for coming, Alice. I knew I could count on you to make Chad feel more a part of the group. You're such a good chaperone that you'll undoubtedly be asked again next year." Vera giggled.

"I'm learning more than the children," Alice said with a small laugh. "These boys speak a foreign language. I have no idea what Game Boys and Pokémon cards are. In my day, the boys played softball and football and games with marbles."

"They still play lots of sports, but some are more computer savvy than I am. It's a different world, but children are still the same. They want to be accepted by their peers, and you've given Chad a big boost today."

A loud noise erupted above them. Chad had been the first to reach the top, and he thrust his fists skyward with a shout of triumph. In a moment he was joined by others, and

soon every fifth grader was punching the air with outstretched arms. Mr. Nichols lagged a bit, but soon he was
standing beside Caitlin, both red-faced and laughing with
arms above their heads.

The other chaperones were still at the halfway point, and
Vera looked at Alice.

"Shall we?" she asked.

"Let's see if all our morning walks will pay off," Alice said
with a grin.

Seventy-two steps were a lot, she decided as she breath-
lessly reached the summit only two steps behind Vera. The
children still hadn't tired of mock boxing, and Chad was at
the center of a group of boys. With animated gestures, he was
retelling the story of the underdog Rocky. It was the first time
Alice had seen him look happy, and it did her heart good.
She had to gasp for air by the time she reached the summit,
and her calves felt as though they'd been tied in knots. Still,
she would have gladly climbed another seventy-two steps to
see Chad's gleeful expression.

Much to Alice's surprise, the group of boys around Chad
gave a little cheer when she crested the top.

"This was a great idea," Matt said to her.

"I'm gonna get my dad to rent the movie," Andrew said.

"I think my uncle Steve has it," Alex said. "I'll borrow it
from him, and you guys can come to my house to see it. You
too, Chad."

Alice turned away to hide her smile. She wasn't worried
about losing Chad on the rest of the trip.

Vera and Caitlin rounded up the group and started them
back down the stairs at a reasonably sedate pace. The fact
that everyone arrived at the bus without plunging downward
and receiving grievous bodily injuries was yet another tribute
to the handling skills of their teacher. Alice hadn't anticipated
the mad stampede up the steps or the possible consequences

of racing down them, so she had to admire how her friend managed to get them back on the bus with every student accounted for and with no bloodied knees.

Mr. Boswell, who smiled at their antics but had not joined in the rush to the top, was congenial about the stop-over and managed to get them on their way. A driver who only made runs in the vicinity of Acorn Hill might have been less able to navigate the heavy, big-city traffic, but he took the unplanned detour in stride.

The bus was buzzing with conversation, and Alice looked over at her seatmate. Chad nodded at her and said, "Thanks. That was cool."

hadn't had the heart to clear everything of their father's out of the desk. Jane found what she wanted in a bottom drawer under a box of paper clips and a package of envelopes. Father's five-year daily calendar, a rather large book covered in red leather, had entries up to his last weeks of life. She slowly worked her way back to the time when he was still active in the life of the congregation.

All his appointments were carefully noted on the appropriate days, and she found familiar names and ones that were unknown to her. After skimming through a number of entries, she noticed that one name appeared with some regularity. Her father had had lunch dates and shared other activities with another minister, Rev. Louis Granger. Jane vaguely remembered him from when she was a child. Her father had been a mentor to him when Rev. Granger was first called to a church in Potterston. Apparently, their ministries had been the basis of a longtime friendship.

Was Rev. Granger still living? He was at least ten to twenty years younger than Jane's father and could well be.

Did Rev. Thompson have a friend within the ministry, someone who served as his mentor? Jane didn't know, but she did know that everyone needed to confide in a peer when making serious decisions. She was doubly blessed in having her two sisters in addition to the friends she'd made since returning to the town, but did their pastor have anyone outside the Grace Chapel congregation in whom he could confide?

The back of her father's daily book had pages for addresses, and she found Louis Granger's phone number there. Would she be overstepping the boundaries of friendship if she intervened on her friend's behalf? She wasn't sure, but she also doubted that he really wanted to leave the chapel. He needed more guidance than she knew how to give.

Uneasy about her decision, she went to the phone at the registration desk. She wasn't exactly sure what to say to Rev. Granger, but a plan was slowly forming in her mind.

He answered the phone himself, and she remembered Alice's once mentioning that his wife had succumbed to cancer quite a few years before.

"Rev. Granger, this is Jane Howard." She was going to explain that she was Daniel Howard's daughter, but the man on the other end didn't give her a chance.

"Of course, you're Daniel's little girl, the youngest of his three daughters. What a pleasant surprise to hear from you."

"I hope you still think that when you hear why I'm calling," she said with a nervous laugh.

"I'm glad to hear from you for any reason. Your father was a wonderful friend from the time I first came to Potterston straight from seminary."

Encouraged by his kind words, she asked that he keep what she was going to say confidential. He readily agreed, and she explained that Acorn Hill was in danger of losing its minister.

"It's not that I would oppose his leaving if he feels called to do the Lord's work in another capacity," she said, struggling for just the right words to explain her concerns. "But I want to be sure that he realizes how important he is to Grace Chapel. He's made such a difference in so many lives here."

"I see." He was quiet for several moments, and Jane didn't know how to interpret his lack of response. Then he said, "Your father said many good things about your training as a chef, Jane. Is there any chance you might have time to fix a meal for an old man who gets very tired of his own cooking?"

"I would love to."

"And, while you're going to all that trouble, you might ask another guest, say your Rev. Thompson."

"Yes, I'll do that. I'll certainly do that."

"Set a date that works for your minister and let me know. My social calendar isn't crowded these days except on Saturday, when I work at the soup kitchen here in town."

After Jane had thanked Rev. Granger and hung up, she immediately called the church office to see whether Rev. Thompson was available for dinner anytime soon. She didn't know what would come of bringing him together with her father's longtime friend, but she felt optimistic for the first time since he'd returned from the job interview.

∽

The traffic in Philadelphia had thinned a bit now that the noon-hour rush was over, and the ride to the zoo wasn't long. Alice kept an eye on her wristwatch, but she needn't have worried. Mr. Boswell managed to arrive at the zoo parking lot only minutes after the time Mark was expecting them. Vera made quick work of getting the children off the bus and shepherded toward the administration building, where they were to meet Mark.

He came outside to greet the group, and he wasn't alone. A young man in blue cotton scrubs was directly behind him with an animal carrier.

"I'm afraid it's my fault that we're late," Alice said, walking toward her tall, distinguished friend with the graying beard and white hair at his temples.

Mark had worn a bright red polo shirt with his khaki slacks, maybe so it would be easy for the children to keep him in sight as they toured the zoo. He greeted Alice with a warm smile and a handshake.

"It's good to see you. This is Dr. Steve Case," he said, indicating the young man beside the carrier.

"You've met Vera Humbert, Mark," Alice said, smiling at the two vets.

"Yes, and I've heard wonderful things from Alice about your work at the school," Mark said graciously, shaking hands.

Vera quickly introduced the other chaperones, then stepped back so Mark could satisfy the children's curiosity about the amber-eyed feline face peering out at them from the thick mesh of the animal carrier.

"This is Duke, a male lion cub. He managed to get into some trouble and hurt one paw. We had to keep him isolated to give it time to heal, but he's a rambunctious one. He can't wait to get back to his pride, the group of lions that he lives with."

"Can you take him out of his cage?" a boy at the back of the group asked.

"Not here. We might have quite a time catching him if he got loose, but you can have a closer look if you want to line up and see him one at a time," Mark said, stooping beside the carrier that Dr. Case placed on the ground. "Have you ever been this close to a lion before?"

The children made it clear that they hadn't.

"You'll notice that he's only beginning to show signs of growing the mane that all males have. He'll lose the little spots you can still see on his head. He was born with soft, woolly, yellowish-gray fur, but he'll be tawny colored when he's an adult."

"How long does it take for a cub to mature?" Mr. Nichols, the twins' father, asked.

"About thirty months."

"Why did you name him Duke?" a girl asked.

"The lion is considered to be royalty among wildlife, so we gave him a title as a name. His brothers are Baron and Earl, and his sister is Duchess."

One by one, the children stooped to go eyeball to eyeball with the cub.

"If he was loose, would he bite?" Andrew asked, taking his turn to stare into the carrier.

"I never guarantee what a wild creature will do, but it's unlikely at this stage that Duke would do more than playfully nip. Lion cubs love to play. In fact, that's how they learn the hunting skills they need to survive. I never get tired of

She had to think for a moment. Then she nodded. "You know, I actually am. I wasn't sure for a while, but it's fun to see things through the eyes of ten- and eleven-year-olds."

Mark stopped in front of the polar bear exhibit in Bear Country and waited for the group to quiet down before resuming his talk.

"At the Philadelphia Zoo, we take pride in providing a habitat that meets the needs of our animals. The polar bears are a good example of this."

A huge white bear splashed into the water behind him, riveting the children's attention.

"What do they eat?" a voice called out.

"They're carnivores. Do you know what that means?"

"Hot dogs for dinner," a would-be comic called out.

"Close enough. They live on meat, just like Duke and his lion pals. That means a polar bear in the wild has to hunt seals and other smaller animals. Sometimes they get lucky and find a whale or a walrus carcass to feast on, but they don't belong to the clean-plate club. Usually they leave enough behind to feed smaller animals like the fox."

"Do they hibernate?" one of the chaperones asked.

"Only the females, but the males go through a period of walking hibernation where their heart rate and breathing are slower. Who can tell me what color polar bear fur is?"

Several children called out, "White."

"It looks sort of yellow to me," Alex said skeptically.

"Actually, it's neither," Mark said with a smile. "Each individual hair is a clear hollow tube that channels the sun's energy to the bear's skin. It's a way to stay warm in extremely cold temperatures. It only appears to be white like the coat of a rabbit or a house cat. Here's another odd thing: The polar bear even has fur on the bottom of its paws to keep it from slipping on ice. It's a great swimmer too, as you can see here. Its feet are partially webbed, and its fur is water-repellent.

You could say that it's a natural wet suit. The polar bear is so much at home in the water that it's classified as a marine mammal."

"How much do they weigh?" The girl who asked was a bit on the pudgy side, and Alice was glad that none of the other students made an unkind remark about her question.

"Normal weight for a female is three hundred fifty to six hundred pounds, although they have been known to weigh a hundred pounds more. Papa Bear is a real heavyweight. Typically, he weighs from five hundred to one thousand pounds, but a really huge bear can weigh as much as 1,500 pounds and be eleven feet long. Polar bears and Kodiak bears are the largest four-footed carnivores on earth. I've spent my whole life working with wild animals, and they still take my breath away sometimes because they're so magnificent."

He didn't need to tell them that polar bears were also immensely entertaining. Alice was fascinated by the glimpse Mark had given into their world, and the children had to be gently prodded into moving on to the next exhibit.

Alice knew that even a full day, let alone an afternoon, wasn't enough time to properly enjoy all that the Philadelphia Zoo had to offer, so she wasn't surprised when Mark elected to bypass a whole area devoted to birds, reptiles and small mammals. Large mammals, especially elephants, were his specialty, and the children seemed to share his enthusiasm for nature's giants.

She'd always been fascinated by the rhinoceros. It amazed her that a beast could get so huge—Mark said four thousand to six thousand pounds—on a diet of leaves and grass. Its huge head and fibrous horn seemed to belong in the age of dinosaurs, and she marveled that the alien-looking creature had survived in the modern world.

"These are black rhinos," Mark told the group, stopping to give them time to look. "We have a separate exhibit of white rhinos on the other side of the park, but don't expect them to look white to you. The biggest difference from the black rhino is a wider mouth. In South Africa, the Dutch settlers call it a *weit* mouth, meaning wide. Early English settlers misinterpreted *weit* for *white*, and that name stuck."

Alice was sure that no trip to the zoo would be complete without a visit to the great apes, and Mark included lots of time on his tour to enjoy them. Philadelphia's Primate Reserve was more fun than—well, a barrel of monkeys. Some of the children had seen the movie *King Kong* and were fascinated to see real gorillas.

"I thought they were bigger," Chad said a bit critically. "How tall are they?"

"An adult male is around five foot five to five foot nine, but he can weigh over three hundred pounds. Females weigh about half that. If you boys were gorillas, your hair would start to turn silver pretty soon. After about age twelve, the male gorillas are called silverbacks because their fur lightens. In the wild, the dominant male is the leader of a troop of up to thirty gorillas. He makes all the decisions about where to go and what to do."

"So that's why they call King Kong a king," Chad said with satisfaction.

Alice was ready to sit down with a nice cup of tea and rest her feet, but the children's enthusiasm hadn't waned. She hoped Mark had allowed enough time to answer all their questions and still see the major exhibits, but, of course, he'd already demonstrated how good he was with children.

They were skirting around Bird Lake, where, unfortunately, there wasn't time to allow the children to ride in the swan boats, when a commotion caused her to look back. Four of her boys were clustered around a bush and obviously excited about something.

Her first thought was that they'd found a snake. Then she laughed at herself for her instant of panic. She hurried over to them, noticing that Matt was hanging back from the other four.

"There's another one!" Andrew cried out.

Her group was separating, going off in different directions, and that wasn't good. Erik had something cradled in his arm, and she fervently hoped it wasn't something that bit, scratched or slithered.

"Oh my!" she exclaimed.

Erik straightened and shouted an order to Andrew, Chad and Alex. Amazingly, they were quick to follow it.

"Boys, stay together!" she called out, but it was obvious that Erik was already calling the shots.

Her boys had been bringing up the rear, and the rest of the children were getting well ahead of them. She walked over to Erik, hoping to enlist his help in rounding up the others so they wouldn't be left behind.

When she saw what he was holding, her jaw dropped.

"What on earth?"

"I found it," he said proudly.

"Here's another one!" Alex called out.

"Bring it here!" Erik ordered.

"I have one too." Andrew stepped back onto the path holding a tiny creature in two outstretched hands.

"Where's Chad?" Alice asked, too concerned about losing track of him to deal with anything else at the moment.

She looked frantically behind the bushes and down the path in both directions.

"Two!" Chad said triumphantly, coming up behind her with both hands full. "I've found two."

"Is that all, do you think?" Erik asked in an earnest voice. "We can't leave any behind. Here, Miss Alice, hold this one. I'll check to be sure."

Alice found herself holding a ball of fur so soft it inspired a wave of tenderness in her. The boys had found a litter of kittens.

"I'm pretty sure that's all," Erik said, returning to the others.

Matt stayed a few feet away, but he obviously wanted to share in the excitement of finding the recently born babies.

"You can probably come closer," Alice assured him. "It's the dander on cats that causes allergic reactions. Kittens this young shouldn't be a problem."

He edged closer with a broad smile, and when she proved to be right, ventured to take one of the two Chad was holding.

"Is there any sign of the mother?" Alice asked.

All the boys replied in the negative.

"Take another look, Erik. Be sure she isn't lurking somewhere nearby."

When he returned without seeing any sign of an adult cat, she took his word for it. She had a strong suspicion about how the kittens had gotten there. They were so tiny, they had no business being away from their mother. But some hardhearted owner must have dumped them.

It made a bizarre kind of sense. Smuggling such tiny creatures into the zoo wouldn't have been much of a challenge. They would easily fit in a backpack, purse or shopping bag. Maybe the owner picked the zoo because it would be filled with animal lovers who might give the kittens new homes. She knew how Viola Reed sometimes struggled to place all the offspring from her large collection of cats.

On the other hand, it was irresponsible and cruel to abandon such young kittens. Alice had some harsh thoughts for any person who would abandon tiny, helpless creatures. They couldn't live long without food and care.

"We'll take them to Dr. Graves," she said in a firm voice. "He'll know what to do with them."

They caught up with the group, but before they could reach Mark, the other children gathered around. More than one begged to hold a kitten, but Erik sternly refused. Vera was equally firm in refusing to let any of the litter go home on the bus with them.

"You can't take home a pet without a parent's permission," she told several children who wanted to adopt one.

Mark frowned when he saw the kittens and heard the boys' story, but he had nothing but praise for their rescue. He made a call on his cell phone, and it wasn't long before a zoo employee came to take them to a safe place.

"What will you do with them?" Andrew asked in a worried voice that suggested they might become food for some fierce carnivore.

"We may have to bottle-feed them for a while, but they'll be safe and well cared for here at the zoo. I'm sure there are people who work here who will be delighted to give the kittens new homes when they're old enough. Thank you for your concern."

Their time was running short, but Mark gave them a quick view of the giraffes and white rhinos, then led them to the Children's Zoo.

"We were the first in North America to have a children's zoo," he said, speaking mostly to the chaperones because the fifth-graders were still buzzing about the great cat rescue. "I know you have to leave soon, but I thought the children would enjoy seeing the Scottish Highland cattle on our farm."

The children spread out, finding sheep and goats to pet, a tractor for climbing and hay for jumping. Vera gave them a play break, but a few stayed near Mark to listen to him talk about the shaggy Scottish cows. Alice thought the hairy beasts with their long, pointed horns were delightful, but she was as pleased as the children when Mark gathered children and grown-ups together and treated them all to cake and ice cream on a patio overlooking the zoo.

"Well, will you be back next year on another fifth-grade

excursion?" Mark asked the adults with a smile as they enjoyed the refreshments together.

"I will if I'm asked," Alice said. For a moment, she was surprised that she had answered so enthusiastically.

"I'll see you long before then," he said. "Thank you for including me in the fun. I'll keep you posted on the fate of the kittens." He bade the group good-bye and gave a warm smile to Alice.

A weary bunch rode back to Acorn Hill on Mr. Boswell's bus. Alice was pleased that Chad had insisted on reclaiming the seat next to her even though Erik and Matt had both made a bid for it.

"Well, what did you like best on the trip?" she asked him when they were underway.

He thought a minute but didn't seem to resent her question.

"I think it was having you as a chaperone."

She knew how it felt to have her cup runneth over.

Chapter Eleven

Jane had a full house to feed for breakfast Tuesday morning, but in this case it only meant four people, all men. Two were engineers sent to inspect a bridge north of town that might need replacing. One was a salesman who made regular stops in Potterston but liked to stay with them in Acorn Hill. The fourth, Mr. Shedow, was a bit mysterious. He was vague about how he'd heard of the inn and made a point of paying cash in advance. She wasn't even sure that he planned to be there for breakfast.

The engineers asked for breakfast at seven, as did the salesman, so the three of them would come down at the same time. The fourth guest kept his plans to himself.

Jane had wanted to try a new recipe for banana bread, and this seemed like a good opportunity. The wonderful spicy aroma would welcome the guests to breakfast, and it was delicious served warm from the oven. For the main course, she opted for omelets. They could be made to order while each guest enjoyed a fruit cup made with yogurt. If the mysterious guest decided against breakfast, she wouldn't be wasting food.

After the bread was in the oven, the coffee started and the fruit cups in the fridge ready to serve, she assembled ingredients for the omelets. She chopped green peppers, onions, mushrooms and ham, then set out grated cheese and a jar of her homemade salsa. In case any of the guests wanted toast, she cut thick slices of cracked-wheat, buttered them and put them on a broiler pan to be oven-toasted.

Breakfast preparations kept her busy but didn't stop her from thinking of the dinner she'd arranged for that evening. Rev. Thompson had seemed a bit surprised by her invitation but was pleased to accept. It remained to be seen whether Rev. Granger would find a way to encourage him to stay at Grace Chapel.

Breakfast was under control, but as a last-minute addition for the omelets, she decided to dice a couple of tomatoes on her cutting board.

"Good morning."

Jane was so startled by the unexpected voice that she nearly nicked her finger with the knife she was using.

"I'm sorry if I startled you," Mr. Shedow said. "I don't eat breakfast as a rule, but I would appreciate a cup of coffee."

"Of course," she said. "If you would like to sit in the dining room, I'll bring it right in."

Their guest was wearing a fashionably cut coal black suit that emphasized how thin he was. His black hair was slicked down on his skull, and his dark eyes were heavily shadowed above sunken cheeks and an unusually sharp nose and chin. If she were casting a vampire movie, he would be a shoo-in.

The timer rang, and she hurriedly removed the banana bread from the oven before taking a small tray with coffee, cream and sugar into the dining room.

"I just took banana bread from the oven if you would like to try it. I'm making omelets for breakfast. There are also fruit cups and cracked-wheat toast."

"Just the coffee, thank you."

By the time the other three men came down for breakfast a few minutes later, her mysterious guest was nowhere to be seen. Apparently, he'd hastily finished his coffee and then left.

The others seemed to be impressed by the menu Jane described, and she started back to the kitchen to prepare the omelets.

"Say, I didn't know I'd be staying in the same inn as a celebrity," the younger of the two engineers, Mr. Ferguson, said. "I saw him on the way out as I was coming down the stairs."

"Celebrity?" Jane didn't have a clue what he meant.

"The spooky-looking guy in the black suit," his older gray-bearded partner, Mr. Osler, said. "My wife has read every book he's written. In fact, I've bought a few myself when I needed a little gift for her. I've seen his face on so many book jackets I would recognize him anywhere."

"Who is he?" Jane asked.

"Desmond McCall Shedow. I don't read much myself, but my wife says they call him the new Dickens. Guess he examines the dark underside of New York City the way Dickens exposed poverty in Victorian England. That's what my wife says, anyway."

"He writes creepy stuff," Mr. Ferguson said, his wide grin and curly red hair making him look like a schoolboy. "But I guess he's made a mint doing it. My wife can't even wait for the paperback editions. She has a standing order at the bookstore for every new book he writes."

"He was probably off to sign books or give a talk, whatever it is authors do." Mr. Osler said. "Darn. I should have gotten his autograph. My wife would've been thrilled."

When the guests had been fed and the last one went upstairs to get ready to leave, Jane walked out to the registration desk. There, to her surprise, was a book with a sleek silver and black cover, the title and author's name spelled out in brilliant crimson letters: *The Ghost of Marley* by Desmond McCall Shedow.

She opened it and was even more surprised. He'd written: "To the very hospitable ladies of Grace Chapel Inn. I enjoyed my stay amid the Victorian splendor of your domicile, and no doubt, like Marley's ghost, I shall return. D. McCall Shedow."

"What are you reading?" Louise asked as she came down the steps and saw Jane by the desk.

"We had a famous guest and didn't know it," Jane said with a laugh. "Look at this."

"My goodness," Louise said after she read the inscription.

"The engineers recognized him, even though they don't read his books. Their wives are avid fans. Have you heard of him?"

"He sounds vaguely familiar. Maybe Viola has his book in stock, although it's not her kind of literature," Louise said thoughtfully, "This doesn't look like something I would read either. If the blurb on the book jacket isn't exaggerating, it must be a frightening story."

"Apparently they call him the new Dickens. He's good at depicting the unattractive side of life."

"Well, he certainly borrowed the Marley in his title from Dickens. I believe I'll stick with the old Dickens. I enjoyed *A Christmas Carol* far more than I expected. There have been so many versions that I've encountered over the years that I expected to find it tiresome. It's anything but. I love the part where Scrooge's nephew says that his uncle's wealth is no use to him because he doesn't do any good with it. You might enjoy reading it yourself."

"Maybe I will."

"I left the copy Viola lent me in Father's library, but he had a copy of his own too. If you do read it, perhaps you'd like to come to the meeting of the book group when they discuss it."

"I might come for one meeting, although I doubt that I'll become a regular member. I am curious to see how Sarah's plum pudding goes over. If I help her serve it, I'll have a good excuse for being there," Jane said.

"Well, I hope you don't regret offering to help her make it." Louise smiled to soften her warning.

∽

Louise and Jane had finished their own omelets when Alice came into the kitchen.

"Good morning, sleepy head," Louise said. "Your big trip must have worn you out."

"I was tired, but I had a wonderful time."

Jane told Alice about their celebrity guest as she fixed an omelet for her.

"It's amazing what interesting people show up when you open your door to visitors," Alice said. "I've never once regretted turning our home into a bed-and-breakfast. Oh, and before I forget, the hospital called me to work this afternoon. A nurse in pediatrics is sick, and they're awfully shorthanded. So don't plan on me for dinner."

"Actually, I'm having guests for dinner," Jane said, "and, of course, I'd like to have you with us. Do you remember Rev. Granger, Louis Granger? He used to have a church in Potterston."

"Certainly! He was a close friend of Father's," Alice said. "I'm sorry I won't be here to see him."

"Nor will I, unfortunately," Louise said. "When I finish my lessons this afternoon, I'm going to Potterston to meet a friend for dinner, Liz Frederickson. You may remember her, Alice. We graduated from high school in the same class, and we've wanted to get together for some time. She called last night, and as much as I'd like to see Rev. Granger again, I won't be able to cancel."

"Oh, that's too bad," Jane said. "Actually, I'm also having a second guest. Kenneth is coming."

"What makes me think that there's more to this invitation than seeing an old friend?" Louise asked.

"I hope I'm not being devious," Jane said with a worried look, "but I thought maybe Kenneth would like to talk to an older minister, someone who may have faced the kind of choice he's facing."

"Does Rev. Granger know why he's invited?" Louise asked.

"Yes. In fact, dinner was his idea, but I have to admit that I called him for advice about Kenneth."

"I hope their meeting has a positive result," Louise said. "But don't worry. I'm sure Rev. Granger will know what to say to Kenneth so that it doesn't seem that he's interfering."

"I think it's wonderful that you're so concerned, Jane," Alice said. "I'm sure Kenneth won't mind even if he does realize why you invited him. He's sensible enough to accept help wherever it's offered."

"Well, I'm sorry neither of you will be here to back me up," Jane said. "But maybe it will work out better that way. I'll find an excuse to leave the two of them alone for a while. Calling Father's old friend was all I could think to do. There's really nothing I can say to Kenneth that will persuade him to stay."

"Well, I have a full day," Louise said, getting up from the table. "If you don't have any jobs that you need me to do right now, I'm going to Nine Lives."

"Remind Sarah that I'm expecting her tomorrow morning, and that you said you would watch the bookstore while we make plum pudding."

"Yes, I will," Louise said. "When Sarah gets an idea, I'd rather be as far away from it as possible. But don't let me spoil your fun. I'm sure you'll enjoy working together."

Louise walked toward Nine Lives at a brisk pace, enjoying another sunny spring day. Trees were budding and new grass was sprouting to replace the drab winter ground cover. It was a perfect day to run errands. She wouldn't stay long at the store today, just the time it would take to put together a bank deposit and make entries in the daily account book.

Louise hoped that she had convinced Sarah not to wander away when she was in charge of the store. It wasn't that the people of Acorn Hill would walk off with books without paying. Rather, when they came in, they had a right to expect someone to be there to help them and answer questions. Viola had made a success of her business by giving personal attention to all her customers. Her enthusiasm for books rubbed off on everyone who knew her.

Louise stopped and took a deep breath before entering the bookstore. She opened the door and forgot to exhale for a moment when she saw what was happening.

Whatever she'd expected, it certainly wasn't the crowd jammed into the relatively small retail space. There were people everywhere, familiar faces and strangers, all of them intently searching the shelves, avidly reading or talking in groups. Three women crowded the checkout counter poring over a single book. Others were sitting on the floor. A young man she recognized as Buck Diesel, Sarah's landscaping friend, was on the rung of a ladder passing books down to waiting hands.

"Louise, you're finally here. We can use your help too." Florence Simpson, dressed in a lavender suit and ruffled white blouse, emerged from behind a freestanding book display.

"Florence, what's going on?"

"I just dropped by to check on the book I ordered," she said. "I'm on my way to a luncheon meeting in Potterston for one of the charities I support. I always like to go early so I have time for shopping first. Ronald is so particular about his socks. They have to be 100 percent cotton. There's only one store that carries them."

"Where's Sarah?" Louise asked quickly before Florence could explain more about her husband's taste in stockings.

"I think she's manning the computer."

"Manning?" Louise said to herself as she hurried toward the back room.

She nearly bumped into Sarah's unofficial assistant, Mr. Trotty. He was wearing a starched white dress shirt, gray flannel trousers and a blue paisley tie, perhaps signs of his elevated position as unpaid helper.

"Mr. Trotty, excuse me," she said, noticing as she passed him that his book of choice was a phone directory.

In the back room, Sarah was hunched over the computer,

busily clicking on entries. She didn't look up as Louise came close and started reading the screen over her shoulder.

"What on earth is going on?" The jumble of words and pictures on the computer meant nothing to her.

"Oh, Mrs. Smith. We have plenty of help on the research, but you can start calling travel agents if you like."

"Are you going somewhere?" She could only hope.

"Oh no, not me. Mr. Trotty."

"What are all those people doing? Why are they here? Sarah, talk to me!"

"Oh, some are customers. I ran a special on gardening books, ten percent off. Ms. Reed won't mind. It did bring a few people into the store." She clicked the mouse several times without looking up.

"All those people are here to buy gardening books?"

"No, they're helping Henry plan his trip."

"Who is Henry?"

"Mr. Trotty."

"Sarah, stop a minute and tell me exactly what's happening here."

"Sorry, I didn't mean to leave you out of the loop, Mrs. Smith. Things have just been happening so fast. Where should I begin?" She still kept half her attention on the screen.

"Start with the reason why all those people are rummaging through books. If they're not all customers—and I can see that some certainly aren't—what are they doing here?"

"Oh, you mean my friend, Buck Diesel. He's still working on the grounds around the town hall. When he saw all the people coming here, he got curious. Don't worry that he'll get in trouble. He's allowed to take a break from work, but he has to leave soon. He has a truckload of shrubs to plant. The town is really trying to spruce up the place. That's a joke he likes to tell. You know, landscaping, sprucing."

Louise unconsciously clenched her teeth, still in the dark about the reason for all the commotion. "Sarah, please."

"I guess the store is pretty crowded," she admitted, turning away from the computer screen to face Louise. "I was talking to Henry. You know, he used to be a librarian. He told me that there are two things he's always wanted to do. Guess what they are."

"Just tell me." Louise insisted, silently praying for patience.

"He's always wanted to eat fresh salmon caught in an Irish stream and baked in cream."

Louise had no idea how Irish salmon differed from any other—or what it had to do with the bedlam in the store.

"And?"

"And he's always wanted to see the *Book of Kells*. It's this book that Celtic monks made centuries ago. Henry explained it all to me. The *Book of Kells* has the four gospels, and the thing is, they drew these little pictures on every page. It's supposed to be the most beautiful book ever made."

"Yes, I know what the *Book of Kells* is."

"Henry said it's also called the *Book of Columbus*."

"I think you mean *Columba*," Louise said, although she didn't know where she'd learned that bit of information.

"Anyway," Sarah went on enthusiastically. "The book is on display at a college library in Ireland."

"Trinity College, Dublin," Louise said to speed up her story.

"They only display one page at a time in a locked case like in a museum, and no one can touch it. I just read on the Internet that they sent part of it, the book of Mark, to Australia for a special exhibition not long ago. The paint— the pigments, I should say—were slightly damaged just from riding in a plane with big engines. At least that's what the experts think. I guess it won't be going on any more trips, and that's what everyone is doing here."

Louise stared at her blankly.

"Henry has always wanted to see it, and that can only happen in Ireland. Also the salmon thing. Boy, I would never eat anything cooked in cream. I could kiss my modeling career good-bye for sure. I asked him why he hasn't gone. I mean, he has a pension and whatever. He can afford to go. He certainly has time. I mean, how boring can his life be if he comes in here every day to look at a fish book?"

"Why doesn't he go?" Louise knew she had to ask if she ever wanted to know what was happening.

"He doesn't have anyone to go with. He's sort of outlived most of his friends. That's really sad, isn't it? So I told him he should go with a group, you know, on a tour. He can make new friends, and he's really healthy for his age, all that bike riding. There's really no reason not to go. So we're helping him."

"All those people?" Louise pointed at the crowd in the front part of the store.

"Well, a lady came in to buy a book for her aunt's birthday, and she got interested in Henry's plan to go to Ireland. Actually, it was still my plan for him to go then, but he was warming to the idea. She mentioned a bus tour that she'd taken. Then Mrs. Simpson came, and she suggested we should ask other people for ideas, so she called the library on her cell phone."

"The librarian is here?"

"No, she couldn't leave her job, but the Friends of the Library were just finishing their meeting, so some of them came over to give us ideas. Then one of them went to the Coffee Shop to find a friend, and more people came. One couple said they went to Ireland for their fortieth wedding anniversary. They gave Henry lots of ideas about places to see. Imagine, they have a castle where you can eat with your hands just like in the old days. It's something ratty. Yeah, Bunratty Castle. Wow! Henry is going to have a hot time."

Louise was stunned, and she was especially concerned about Mr. Trotty. Was he being carried away by Sarah's enthusiasm and the crowd of helpers who'd assembled in the store? Or did he really intend to go to Ireland?

She found him poring over the pages of a book along with a woman who was best known for her crusade to ban automobiles on the streets of Acorn Hill.

"I'm very disappointed that there doesn't seem to be a tour you can take by horse-drawn carriage," the back-to-nature enthusiast said. "You could get a real feeling for the way people used to live, the way they would still live if automobiles weren't polluting the earth. No matter, there should be opportunities to hike and camp. I hear Ireland is incredibly beautiful with bright green hills like nowhere else. They don't call it the Emerald Isle for nothing."

"I'm sure they don't," Louise said, managing to draw Mr. Trotty off to the side in an area of children's books that hadn't been overrun by his enthusiastic helpers. "Now, Mr. Trotty, is this something you really want to do?"

"Yes, Sarah is right. I should realize my dream before I get too old."

"And all these people are helping you?"

He grinned, and even the network of wrinkles on his face seemed to smile. "Let them have their fun. I'm going to have mine as soon as I can book a tour. Sarah is right about not going on my own. Life is a journey. Why not take the long way 'round and meet new people on the way?"

Louise had just heard words repeated twice that she'd never expected to hear at all: "Sarah is right."

"I guess we all have our dreams," Mr. Trotty said a bit sheepishly.

Louise thought of her longtime fantasy of visiting all the cathedrals and opera houses in Europe where the music of great composers like Beethoven, Bach and Mozart was first performed.

"Yes, we do," she said, smiling broadly at the elderly man and seeing him differently. "Well, what can I do to help?"

"If I had any more help, it would be enough to launch me to the moon," he said with a chuckle. "When the excitement dies down, I'll get myself over to a travel agent in Potterston to see what needs to be done."

"Good plan."

"She's quite a girl, young Sarah. If I were fifty years younger, I'd marry her."

"Quite a girl," Louise agreed, wondering what she herself could or should do to restore sanity to Nine Lives.

Eventually all the "visitors" drifted out of the store, nearly half of them buying books before they left. The rummaging for travel hints had unearthed books that browsers often overlooked. Louise took care of selling and bagging the purchases. Sarah was much too busy researching on the computer, trying to find the best tour for Mr. Trotty.

∽

Jane still wondered about the wisdom of bringing the two ministers together, but she distracted herself by planning a rather elaborate dinner. She always thought it was better to work than fret.

Because the object of the meal was to give them a chance to talk, she decided to begin with an appetizer tray served in the parlor while she prepared the rest of the dinner. She opted for an assortment of seafood specialties that she'd often used when she worked as a restaurant chef. They were so tasty that she couldn't resist trying some before she put them in the fridge. Generally, she avoided the tasting trap. Nibbling as she cooked was a sure way of adding unwanted pounds.

She also decided to try a recipe that Nia Komonos, the town librarian, had been kind enough to share with her. It was her family recipe for moussaka, a treat for which they were justly praised. It was the perfect entrée to carry out her plan, because it would allow her last-minute preparations that would leave the two men alone.

A French bread would be a fitting complement for the

main course, Jane thought, so she decided to avail herself of the wonderful loaves provided by Good Apple Bakery.

She wanted to serve a light dessert. She baked butter cookies to accompany a lemon sorbet. Served in sherbet glasses, it was light and pleasantly tart, the simplest possible end to dinner.

Just to make the meal seem more special, she made an effort to dress up more than usual. She saw an opportunity to wear her dove gray linen slacks with a silver link belt and a turquoise short-sleeved sweater tucked into the waistband. She coiled her hair in an upswept style and chose dangly silver and turquoise earrings to complete her outfit.

Their minister would soon realize her purpose for inviting him. He would know her stylish outfit and gourmet cooking were only a front for the meeting with Rev. Granger. She silently prayed that he would forgive her if the evening turned into an uncomfortable counseling session with the older man, and she wished that at least one of her sisters could be there to support her.

Rev. Granger arrived first, which proved to be a blessing for Jane's peace of mind. He was short and a bit rotund, and he radiated good humor and warmth from the moment he stepped into the inn. His hair was snowy white and still thick enough to cover his head, and his mustache was the same color. He wore small, round metal-framed glasses and tended to look over the top of them when he talked.

"Jane, I can't tell you what a pleasure it is to see you again. You probably don't remember the time when your father and I took you for your first pony ride on my granduncle's farm."

"I'm afraid not," she said regretfully, unable to place the minister in her childhood memories.

"After that, Daniel and I were both so busy with our churches and families that we didn't have time for pony rides. A shame really, but your father and I were very close in later years. I still miss his companionship and wonderful sense of humor."

"Thank you," she said, feeling a pang of regret that her father was no longer with them.

Rev. Thompson soon arrived, and after introducing the two men, Jane settled them in the parlor with her tray of appetizers and the goblets of mineral water they had requested.

"Everything has to be done at the last minute," she explained. "Please make yourselves at home."

She didn't hurry, but the suspense about what was happening gnawed at her as she cooked. Her preparations filled the kitchen with the fragrances of oregano, garlic and cinnamon. As a result of distractions, the rolls browned more than she liked. She expected perfection from herself and hated anything less in her meals. At least the moussaka pleased her, and she was ready to serve dinner to the two ministers.

"That was the most delightful dish I've had in ages," Rev. Granger said after a meal spent discussing neutral topics such as food, weather and his memories of her father. "Such a perfect blending of spices!"

Jane enjoyed herself, but she wasn't sure that Rev. Thompson did. He participated in the conversation but his mind seemed to be elsewhere. After dinner, he was the first to excuse himself and leave, shaking hands with Rev. Granger and offering him a warm good-bye.

"The dinner was delicious, Jane, I'm sure one couldn't find moussaka that good in Athens itself. I haven't had a meal that satisfying in ages. I'm sorry I have to run. I need to make a hospital visit in Potterston this evening, and I don't like to disturb patients when it's late."

"I'm glad you could come." She didn't know what else to say.

"My pleasure."

When Rev. Thompson was gone, she didn't know what

her father's old friend might have to say. Would he tell her how his conversation with her pastor had gone? Or would he treat it as confidential counseling?

"I'm afraid I've put you to a lot of trouble cooking for me when I haven't been very helpful," he said, assisting her in clearing away the dishes from the dining room table.

"Not at all. I loved talking about Father and knowing more about his good friend. I hope you'll come again."

"I would love to, but I'm not sure if Rev. Thompson will be here to join us."

"Oh." She didn't know what to say. Had Grace Chapel's beloved minister decided to leave?

"I don't believe he's made his decision, but I don't think I influenced him one way or the other. At my age, I see life as a journey with peaks and valleys. Everyone has to chart his own course, and sometimes the counsel of the elderly is of no help."

"I'm sure you were a great help," she was quick to respond.

"Perhaps I gave him a few things to consider, but I'm not certain. He talked about the decision, and he knew that prayer could be a true guide for him. Anyway, it has been a great pleasure to see you again, Jane. Thank you for the delicious dinner."

Later, Jane went up to her room without loading the dishwasher or scrubbing pans, a rarity since her return to Acorn Hill to run the inn with her sisters. In her room, she prayed that Rev. Granger's visit would prove to have a positive effect.

Chapter  Twelve

Jane sat up in bed, startled by a horrendous burst of thunder. A moment later lightning illuminated the room, making her curtains seem transparent. She pulled up the covers to her chin.

As a child, she'd been excited by storms. She used to watch from the parlor window as lightning lit up the sky and thunder rumbled in the distance. She loved the story of Rip van Winkle, and when she was very little, she'd been convinced that thunder was the sound of mysterious little men bowling in the mountains.

Now she saw storms differently. One of this intensity could snap branches and knock over whole trees, felling them on roofs and cars. Part of her wanted to crawl under the blanket and return to her dreams, but she was a responsible homeowner now. The inn was particularly vulnerable in a heavy wind because it rose three stories and had a number of ancient trees in the vicinity that could damage the old building. She should be on the alert for sounds of breakage.

She crawled out of bed and went to the window, still fascinated to look out at nature showing its power. Her eyes followed a brilliant flash of lightning across the sky. At the same instant, a movement in the room startled her.

"Wendell," she whispered as the cat rubbed against her ankle.

The black-striped gray tabby could be an independent rascal, but storms turned him into a needy kitty. She reached down and scooped him up, glad that she'd left her door cracked so he could come to her for comfort.

She carried him to her bed and sat on the edge, stroking him between his ears to calm him. The alarm clock on the bedside table showed that it was a few minutes before three AM, an odd time to be comforting a cat and listening to a storm. No doubt, when the storm ended, Wendell would be content to return to his own bed, but she was wide awake now. She knew from experience that it could take hours for her to get back to sleep.

Was anyone else awake? Her sisters were good at sleeping through disturbances, or at least they rarely mentioned sleeplessness if they experienced it. The inn had only two guests this evening, a couple from Connecticut on a leisurely trip to visit relatives in the Midwest, sightseeing along the way.

Jane listened hard between bursts of thunder, but there were no stealthy footsteps to suggest that she wasn't the only one awake. Unfortunately, she was wide-eyed and alert.

She put Wendell down, found her white satin slippers and green Mandarin-style robe and started down the stairs. With only a night-light in the upper hallway to guide her, she managed to avoid the creaky spots on the stairs. If her sisters and their guests were sleeping through the storm, she certainly didn't want to wake them. Wendell streaked ahead of her, ensuring that she wouldn't stumble over him, and by the time she got to the first floor, he'd disappeared.

Warm milk had never appealed to her, whatever its soothing effect, so she made a cup of decaffeinated tea and sat to drink it. The storm was receding, the thunder a distant rumble now, but it was much too early to begin breakfast preparations. When she finished her tea, she wandered out to the library and went inside.

Closing the door behind her, she turned on a reading lamp beside one of the chairs, remembering that Louise had left a copy of Dickens's *A Christmas Carol* in the room. She found it quickly on the desktop and settled down to read a bit. If anything could put her back to sleep, it should be a story retold so often that there couldn't possibly be any surprises in it. She curled up in comfort and expected that she would soon be napping.

"Marley was dead: to begin with," the opening sentence said.

Just to be sure that the reader was absolutely certain, the second paragraph was a single sentence: "Old Marley was dead as a door-nail."

Who knew that old expression came from as far back as Dickens's time? Jane continued reading. In very short order, Scrooge showed his miserly ways to his poor clerk and two gentlemen soliciting for charity. He convinced his well-meaning nephew that Christmas meant nothing to him. It angered Scrooge that he was expected to pay for a day's work and receive no labor for it.

When the miserly old man returned to his dismal lodgings and saw Marley's face on the door knocker, Jane was hooked. She was fascinated by the details of his living quarters, especially the old fireplace surrounded by Dutch tiles illustrating the Scriptures. She reveled in the ringing, clanking, dragging sounds that assailed Scrooge, and loved it when he attributed the vision of Marley to "an undigested bit of beef, a blot of mustard, a crumb of cheese, a fragment of an underdone potato."

She laughed out loud when Scrooge said to the ghost, "There's more of gravy than of grave about you, whatever you are."

By then she could no more put down the book than

Scrooge could stop the ghostly visitations. She was awed by the talent of a writer whose words still enchanted after more than a hundred fifty years.

When Scrooge, at last, embraced the spirit of Christmas and became a better man, Jane felt that she'd been on an inspirational journey. She read Tiny Tim's closing words, "God bless us, every one!" with tears in her eyes.

Fortunately, *A Christmas Carol* was more a long short story than a novel. Once started, there was no putting it down, and she finished the last page just as the first hints of dawn started showing through the library windows.

She thanked God for the genius of great authors and for the storm that had brought her to the library. Afterward, she remained seated, thinking. At the back of her mind, the germ of an idea was forming. Maybe, just maybe, there was a message for her in the tale she'd just read.

For now, she had breakfast to prepare. She hurried upstairs to shower and dress, feeling so energized that she forgot about her interrupted sleep.

∽

Louise made her way toward the kitchen before their guests came down for breakfast. She'd promised to work at the bookstore while Sarah made plum pudding with Jane, but before she went to Nine Lives, she had to work on the details of her students' upcoming recital. It would be held at Grace Chapel, as usual, but she had to coordinate refreshments, arrange for printed programs and find parents to assist. When that was done, she needed to pay bills and arrange for an electrician to fix the light at the bottom of the inn's cellar steps before one of them stumbled descending the dark stairway.

Jane was there ahead of her, humming to herself as she removed a pan of boiled eggs from the stove.

"You sound chipper this morning," Louise said. "Did you sleep through the storm?"

"No, I came down to the library and read *A Christmas Carol*. I had no idea it was so engrossing. Dickens is the Rembrandt of writers."

"You read the whole story in the middle of the night? You must be exhausted."

"Not at all. In fact, I'm full of energy. The book gave me an idea, but it's too soon to tell you about it. I have to give it a lot more thought."

Louise smiled, all too familiar with her sister's enthusiasms. They often meant that she was ready to embark on a new project, but Louise couldn't imagine what it might be.

"I'll just get myself a bowl of cereal," she said.

"I'm making curried eggs for the guests. I boiled extra eggs if you'd like one."

"No, thank you. Cereal will be fine. Do you think our guests will like curry?"

She rarely questioned Jane's menu choices, but curry in the morning didn't appeal to her at all.

"They mentioned having an exchange student from India when we were chatting yesterday. They've developed quite a taste for exotic food. Curried eggs should be right up their alley."

"Sorry, I should have trusted your judgment." Louise found a box of corn flakes and poured out a small helping. "Are you ready for Sarah?"

"I'm still chuckling about Mr. Trotty's trip to Ireland. She really did a good thing there, didn't she? I wish I'd been there to see half the town trying to plan it for him."

"Florence was the one who rallied the troops, but I give Sarah credit for convincing Mr. Trotty that he could realize his dream. I wonder what the future will hold for her. It definitely won't be a career in retail sales."

"Maybe she'll become a travel agent," Jane said, only half serious.

"I would hesitate to leave on a trip knowing that she'd

made the arrangements, but maybe I'm selling her short. Perhaps she'll do a splendid job on the plum pudding. Thank you again for volunteering to help her."

"It will be fun," Jane assured her.

∞

Jane's mind was too full of her partly formulated idea to stay focused on plum pudding, but she would keep her promise to help Sarah. After the guests left, she cleaned up and started setting out the spices that she'd agreed to provide. The pudding had to be steamed, and she didn't have a waterproof mold. Instead, she would improvise. She'd saved some tin cans, and she planned to cover them with a double layer of aluminum foil securely tied in place by string. Fortunately, she did have a canning kettle with a rack and a tight-fitting cover that would be perfect for the six hours of steaming necessary to cook the puddings.

Just to satisfy her own curiosity, Jane had done a bit of research on puddings. Once, *pudding* was a generic name for most desserts. In later years, it referred to a cooked or steamed dessert that had been thickened. If Sarah was expecting a soft, creamy pudding that could be spooned into a dish, she was in for a surprise. Plum pudding was firm enough to slice and had more in common with fruitcake than the chocolate pudding most children loved.

Sarah had agreed to come to the inn at nine o'clock. Jane understood that she had to drive from Potterston, so she wasn't unduly concerned when nine fifteen came, then nine thirty, with no Sarah. Had she had a mishap on the way there? Had she forgotten?

Jane kept herself busy with small chores in the kitchen, but she was a bit impatient by ten o'clock when Sarah still hadn't arrived or called. Louise only planned to stay at the store until noon, so Sarah had an obligation to arrive at Nine Lives by then. Jane planned to take care of the steaming, but there were quite a few steps in preparing the pudding.

She walked to the front door of the inn and stared out at the quiet street. If Sarah still planned to come, she had to arrive soon.

Jane was expecting to see her arrive by car, so she didn't pay special attention to the landscaping truck that slowed to a stop in front of the inn. When a tall, leggy girl in bright yellow slacks and a jungle-print top got out of the truck, she remembered what Louise had said about a new boyfriend distracting Sarah.

"Hi," the girl called out, hoisting a bag of groceries on one slender hip.

She hustled up to the porch where Jane was waiting for her and handed off the bag.

"I have one more," she said, traipsing back down the path on improbably high cork-soled wedges.

"No, I'll get it," she called out to a rather burly looking young man in a green shirt.

She returned to the porch carrying a second grocery sack.

"I am so sorry I'm late," she said, sounding more breathless than could be explained by the short trek from truck to inn. "I never dreamed it could be so complicated to shop for plum pudding ingredients. You have no idea how hard it was to explain to the man in the meat department that I wanted suet. Yuck! He gave me a whole pile of this gross white fat. Are you sure we have to use it?"

"We'll cream it in my blender. It will melt as the puddings steam, and you won't even know it's there." Jane led the way inside the inn, cutting off Sarah's lingering look at the young man as his truck roared off.

"I thought you had use of a car," she remarked.

"Yes, my aunt lets me drive hers, but I left it in the town lot. I didn't want to—you know—take up a parking space you might need for guests."

Jane looked back at the empty street, then toward their nearly empty inn parking area. She shook her head but decided not to say anything. Instead, she led her young guest to the kitchen. Louise had warned her that Sarah was a bit flighty, especially where her young man was concerned. At least she was here now, and they could get started.

"Put the sack on the counter," she said. "I printed the recipe off the computer if you'd like to read it to refresh your memory before we begin. It's not as complicated at it seems if we just take it a step at a time."

"I've heard you're a wonderful cook." Sarah sounded sincere, not ingratiating. "And not just from Mrs. Smith, although she said that you're a professional chef. I could never be a chef. It's so hard to get everything done at the same time. I only make meals with one thing, like a bowl of soup. Even then, I'm apt to forget the crackers. Fortunately, if I still want to be a model, eating won't be a big thing in my life. Lettuce is a model's best friend. I made up that saying."

"Aha!" Jane hoped that she seemed properly impressed by the news.

Sarah didn't even glance at the recipe lying on the tabletop. Jane realized that the plum pudding was going to end up being her responsibility. Any help she got from Sarah would be incidental, but perhaps that was best. Jane was used to a one-woman kitchen. She looked at the recipe herself, wondering what little jobs she could give Sarah to keep her out of trouble.

"Let's set out the ingredients in the order we'll need them," she said, indicating a roomy space on the counter.

"Oh, I can do that. It's just like putting books in the right section," Sarah said enthusiastically.

"Sort of," Jane agreed, puzzled by the first item Sarah pulled from the sack.

"The recipe doesn't call for dates."

"Oh, I had raisins on my list, but I never liked them. They taste so nasty, but dates are good. My aunt makes date-nut bars that are out of this world, not that I ever eat sweets anymore."

"You bought dates to substitute for raisins?"

"Yes, they're yummy."

"Sarah, it doesn't work that way. You have to follow the recipe. That means putting in the ingredients it calls for."

Jane picked up the recipe, her enthusiasm rapidly waning.

"We only need one cup of raisins," she said, reading the recipe herself. "I have enough on hand. Did you make any other substitutions?"

"I didn't notice the part about *dark* brown sugar," Sarah said, looking at a folded bit of paper she took from the minuscule shoulder pouch that served as her purse.

Jane lifted a hefty plastic bag of brown sugar from the grocery sack. "You got it right."

"Oh wow! That was lucky. I just grabbed. I didn't know brown sugar came in different shades. Makeup shades are terribly important, of course. Next time I'll know to check sugar shades."

Jane pulled out a long loaf of thick-cut bread for Texas toast.

"They didn't have dry bread," Sarah said apologetically. "I thought thick bread would work just as well."

"We'll dry it in the oven."

Jane felt a little weary, and they hadn't even started the recipe. She blamed it on her short night's sleep, then remembered that Sarah seemed to have the same effect on Louise.

"What do you want me to do?"

Jane took note of her ultralong pointed nails painted a shimmering silver color and ruled out chopping the dried figs. Real or fake, a piece of nail would not be a welcome addition to the pudding.

"You can separate the eggs. The recipe calls for four."

Sarah looked at her blankly.

"Separate the yolks from the whites. We'll need to beat the whites until they're stiff, then fold them into the batter. Put the whites in this deep bowl and the yolks into this one."

"Oh, I get it. Crack the eggs and fish out the yellow part."

"Here, let me show you." Jane quickly separated one egg and stepped aside to let Sarah continue.

On her first try, Sarah broke the yolk and dropped it into the bowl with the egg white.

Jane took a deep breath and explained again. "If there's any yolk in the egg whites, they won't get stiff. Here, why don't I finish, and you can measure one cup of raisins. They need to be lightly floured to keep them from sticking together. Spread them on my cutting board and sprinkle just a little flour over them."

She made quick work of separating the eggs, then turned her attention to drying the bread in the oven and scalding the milk to soak it. Sarah was such a distraction that Jane had to keep consulting the recipe to be sure she was on track.

"How's this?" Sarah asked.

Jane glanced over at the raisins. They'd almost vanished under a thick blanket of flour.

"Oh dear. You had the right idea, but it may be too much of a good thing." Jane's experience supervising other chefs in a restaurant kitchen had taught her to be tactful but firm. "You'll have to put them in my wire strainer and shake out some of the flour."

Jane began finely chopping the dried figs while Sarah did a little dance step in front of the sink as she shook the strainer to remove excess flour. At least she was good-natured and didn't make excuses for her mistakes.

She was still doing a rumba of sorts with the raisins when Jane finished her own task. She went on to chopping the suet into manageable pieces to cream in the blender.

"I think the raisins are done," Jane said. "Here's another job for you. Put these pieces of suet in the blender, then put the cover on tight and set the speed to cream them."

"Touch that fat?" Sarah sounded appalled.

"You can pick it up with a fork."

"Oh, okay." She couldn't have sounded more reluctant if Jane had asked her to load earthworms into the blender.

Jane turned her attention to crumbling the oven-dried bread and adding it to the hot milk. It had to cool before they added the rest of the ingredients, so she read the recipe again to see if there were other little jobs to keep her helper busy. At least for the moment, Sarah seemed fascinated by the action inside the blender.

Jane's usual practice was to measure spices and set them aside before they were needed. She considered letting Sarah do it, but she wasn't at all sure her helper knew the difference between a teaspoon and a tablespoon.

An ear-piercing screech shattered her concentration. Her first thought was that Sarah had put her hand in the blender.

Jane rushed over to see what was the matter and didn't know whether to laugh or cry. Sarah had lifted the cover without turning off the blender with messy but hilarious results. She was spattered with liquefied suet; blobs stuck in her hair and dotted her face and clothing. Jane quickly turned off the power and tried not to lose her cool.

"I wanted to see how it was coming," Sarah said, her face a study in despair. "It's all over me. I have fat on everything."

She certainly had that right. The counter and cupboards —as well as Jane's "helper"—were flecked with small clumps.

"It's in my hair!"

Jane handed her a towel to wipe her face.

"My new blouse is ruined. I never should have worn it to cook."

Big tears rolled down her cheeks.

"It's nothing that can't be fixed," Jane assured her. "Come upstairs with me. You can wash up in my shower. I'll lend you something to wear while I run your clothes through the washer and dryer."

"They'll have grease stains."

"Not when I get my hands on them," Jane assured her. "I'll attack the spots with stain remover right away."

She led Sarah up to her room, gave her towels and waited outside the bathroom until Sarah handed out the spattered outfit. Fortunately, the tags still sewn into the garments indicated that they could be laundered and tumble dried. Jane left a T-shirt and wraparound skirt on the bed for Sarah's temporary use, then carried the soiled clothes downstairs to the laundry room and prepared to tackle the stains. After treating each spot separately, she reached for the detergent box. There was scarcely a teaspoon left. She went to the storage room between the laundry room and kitchen, but there was none there.

The inn required a multitude of supplies, and some were stored in the basement. Because Jane was sure they had a spare box of detergent, she headed toward the basement. As soon as she flicked the switch to go down the cellar steps, she remembered their electrical problem. The light at the bottom of the stairs wasn't working. She crept down with only a dim glow from the kitchen to light her way.

The creaky steps and murky depths of the cellar reminded her of Scrooge's unsavory dwelling and the ghosts he encountered. Of course, she didn't believe in phantoms lurking in the shadows, but the dark played tricks on her consciousness. The old cellar seemed menacing, and she descended uneasily.

With great relief she reached the bottom and managed to find the switch that turned on lights in the basement proper. As soon as she could see the familiar shelving and the furnace and water heater, she felt relieved and laughed at her apprehension. How silly to spook herself. She'd better make sure all the lights in the inn were functional before she read any more Dickens.

Jane found the spare box of detergent and went upstairs to start the wash cycle. Back in the kitchen, she applied herself to the plum pudding and had nearly finished by the time Sarah rejoined her.

She looked like a waif in Jane's outfit, which was much too large. Her hair was still damp, and she looked considerably younger without makeup. Now that the crisis was over, she was apologetic.

"I should have warned you that I'm a disaster in the kitchen."

"Don't worry. There is plenty of suet left, and the puddings are ready to steam. All I need to do is put double layers of foil over the tops and tie them on tightly. The water in the steamer will only come halfway up the cans, but we don't want any splashing onto the pudding."

"That's something I can do," Sarah said, regaining some of her enthusiasm. "I want to be able to say I helped."

"Okay," Jane agreed, fairly sure that the young woman couldn't get into more trouble doing that simple chore.

She assembled rags and her best grease-cutting cleanser and began washing all the surfaces spattered by suet. Sarah was conscientious about covering each can and firmly tying the foil in place. Now, as long as the grease spots came out of her clothes, they should be out of crisis mode.

"Jane, are you home?"

She immediately recognized the familiar voice and went out to the entryway to greet Rev. Thompson.

"I never feel quite right just walking into your home," he said with a broad smile when he saw her.

"We're a business too," she reminded him, returning his smile, greatly relieved that he was so friendly after the dinner she'd arranged with Rev. Granger. "We expect people to walk right in."

"I just stopped by to take a look at the rocker. I should decide how to finish it."

"I removed the last bits of paint. I hope you don't mind."

"Mind? I'm grateful. I haven't been able to find time to work on it since we started."

His cheerful attitude made her hopeful. Was he going to stay at Grace Chapel? She didn't feel it was her place to ask.

"I want to thank you again for the excellent dinner with

Rev. Granger. I'd heard of him, but since he retired before I came here, we hadn't had an opportunity to meet. We had a good conversation."

"I'm glad," she said, still hoping for more. "He was a close personal friend of Father's."

"Yes, he told me how I would have enjoyed meeting your father."

She liked hearing good things about her father, but not now, not when she was in such suspense about the future of the chapel.

"I wonder," she began tentatively, "whether—"

The crash seemed to shake the old house on its foundation. The scream that followed was even more alarming. Jane ran to the kitchen with the minister close behind her.

Tongues of flame shot up from the surface of the stove. Before Jane could even determine what was burning, Rev. Thompson grabbed the extinguisher from its wall holder at the end of the kitchen and doused the fire.

Jane slipped and caught herself on the edge of the counter, then looked down at the floor with dismay. All the water had spilled out of the canning kettle, and so had the cans of pudding dough. Most of the foil lids hadn't survived the impact. The thick mix was spreading through the water like mud pies on rainy pavement.

"That's the most spectacular pot holder fire I've ever seen," the pastor said.

Jane laughed, perhaps a bit hysterically. Sarah cried.

"It's not the end of the world," Jane assured her, putting her arm around the sobbing girl and making hurried introductions. "I've seen professional chefs make bigger messes."

This was an exaggeration, but the situation called for kindness.

"We'll get this cleaned up in no time," Rev. Thompson said, taking off his suit jacket and lifting the kettle from the floor. "Here's a can that survived."

"I never want to see another plum pudding in my whole life," Sarah said. "This was the dumbest idea I've ever had."

"Anyone can have an accident." Jane wasn't at all sure that anyone but Sarah could orchestrate disasters of this magnitude trying to make a dessert, but she was curious. "What on earth happened?"

"I wanted to help, so I was going to put the kettle on to boil. I turned on the burner, but I didn't see the pot holder. It went up in flames, just like that!" She threw her arms up in the air. "When I tried to smother the fire with the kettle, it was too heavy and I dropped it. I ruined everything!"

"Odd that it flared up so quickly," the minister said.

"Not if it was covered with suet," Jane said with resignation, remembering that she had sopped up some of the splatters with the closest thing, a pot holder. "And I share some of the blame."

He looked puzzled but was wise enough not to press for an explanation.

He mopped, she scrubbed and between them they calmed Sarah.

The borrowed skirt was soaked on the bottom, so Jane hurried upstairs to lay out another temporary outfit, leaving Rev. Thompson to assure Sarah that no one was angry with her. When she came back and sent the girl upstairs to change, she turned to the minister with gratitude.

"Thank you so much for helping. Louise warned me that I'd have my hands full with Sarah, but I wasn't prepared for a kitchen catastrophe."

"There should be a sermon in this," he said with a laugh, "but I don't think there's anyone in the Bible quite like your helper."

"Maybe that's a good thing. Sarah works for Viola at Nine Lives. The plum pudding was supposed to be for the book group, but I don't think either of us wants to try mixing up another batch."

"Someone else mentioned that group to me. Yes, I remember. It was Florence Simpson. Something about Dickens."

"They're reading *A Christmas Carol*. That's why Sarah had the idea of serving plum pudding as refreshment."

"I read that story many years ago. In fact, I was so young that the ghosts scared me."

"I read it last night during the storm. It may have affected me a little too."

"Our imaginations can play tricks at any age." He said in a somber tone.

He frowned, and something about his change of mood gave her the courage to ask the question that was tormenting her. She had to know.

"You haven't made your decision yet?"

"No."

"Will you do something for me?"

"If I can."

"Go on a mystery trip."

He looked at her in astonishment. "A mystery trip? Where?"

"You'll have to trust me."

"I do."

"You'll go then?" She'd expected more resistance.

"Yes, but I'll have to check my calendar. Can I let you know when I'm available? I can get back to you this evening to work out the details."

"Yes, of course. That's wonderful! Thank you, Kenneth."

If he hadn't been there for the plum pudding disaster, would she have had the nerve to ask the minister on a mystery trip? It was one thing to have an inspiration and quite another to involve her minister and spiritual mentor in it. She seriously doubted that she would have picked up a phone to issue her invitation.

The Lord did work in mysterious ways. Now it was up to her to carry out the plan.

Chapter Thirteen

Jane had people to contact, phone calls to make, visits to plan.

In spite of her interrupted sleep the previous night, she was too agitated to sleep well. Instead of catching up on lost slumber, she awoke especially early Thursday morning, her mind racing with all the things she had to do.

First, of course, was breakfast. After a number of nights with some rooms unoccupied, the inn had a full house. She had seven adults and two children to feed this morning. If her sisters knew how busy she would be today, they would be seriously concerned. There was a reason, of course, but she wasn't ready to talk about her plans for Rev. Thompson.

What about refreshments for the book group this evening? She'd rashly promised Sarah to take care of them herself, assuring her that it was no problem to make cookies or bars. Usually it wasn't, but today she needed every minute to work on the mystery trip.

The more immediate problem was breakfast, and she had the particular challenge of feeding two preschoolers. She'd been toying with the idea of making eggs chasseur, but perfect poached eggs required a patience she didn't have this morning. Also, the rich sauce might not appeal to the children, so she scrapped that idea. She ran through a mental inventory of the contents of the kitchen and came up with a popular recipe that fit the bill—pancakes.

If the children didn't like them, she could always scramble an egg or bring out cereal. Buckwheat pancakes it would be. She had sausage patties and a bottle of genuine maple syrup. With mixed fruit sections as an opener and hot chocolate as an alternative to coffee, her breakfast should be well received.

The two children, an angelic three-year-old girl with a mop of caramel-brown curls and her four-year-old brother, came down with their parents. The girl refused to taste a pancake even though Jane had made a happy face with butterscotch bits to tempt her. Her brother managed to get himself and everything within reach sticky as he licked the syrup from his pancake. To his parents' credit, they were embarrassed by their children's antics and apologized profusely, blaming the early hour. Before they left the dining room, they thanked Jane for her patience and for her delightful breakfast.

Alice had worked late at the hospital, so Jane didn't expect her help. Louise almost always pitched in when the inn was full, but the remaining guests might arrive at any moment, and there was still no sign of her. Jane was replacing the sticky tablecloth in the dining room when her oldest sister hurried in to help her.

"I can't remember the last time I turned off my alarm and went back to sleep," Louise said. "I'm sorry I wasn't here to help."

"It's okay. You have enough responsibilities without waiting tables."

"Today I do. I'm not at all sure I know how to lead a book group. And I'm so sorry about the fiasco with the plum pudding. I blame myself for not being firm with Sarah. I've become quite fond of her, but I should have anticipated a disaster." She followed Jane back to the kitchen. "What should I do for you?"

"Pour syrup into a clean pitcher. That little boy put his sticky fingers on everything he could reach."

"I do have one bit of good news for you—I hope. Sarah said you volunteered to make a dessert, but she decided to take responsibility for the ruined puddings."

"She's going to make something else? By herself?"

"No, nothing like that. She ordered dessert from the Good Apple Bakery. In fact, she made a very good choice, individual lemon tarts. I'm sure they'll be delicious and easy to serve."

"Good choice," Jane said guardedly, imagining all the things that could happen between the bakery and the bookstore.

"Also, she enlisted her boyfriend Buck to pick up the tarts and take them to Nine Lives. He seems reliable. He's always on hand when Sarah needs him. In fact, I sometimes wonder how much work his employer gets in exchange for the salary that young Mr. Diesel receives."

Jane sighed with relief and turned her attention to the savory sausage still warming in her skillet.

"Are you still coming to the book group tonight?" Louise asked.

Jane was tempted to say no. She had too much to do, and neither Sarah nor her sister needed her. Still, Scrooge's encounter with the ghosts was quite fresh in her memory. She decided that she would very much like to hear what others had to say about Dickens's famous tale.

∞

Louise planned to stay only a few minutes at Nine Lives. Sleeping late had put her behind schedule, and she had lessons this afternoon after school was out. The book group met rather early, at 7:00 PM, since some of the older members preferred not to be out late.

She walked to the store, enjoying the chance to stretch

her legs. The day was as pleasant as a spring day could be. The weather report had promised sunshine and warm temperatures for the rest of the week. Viola's book enthusiasts wouldn't be kept home by inclement weather.

The main thing she had to do today was check on Sarah's preparations for the meeting. Much to her relief, the store was quiet when she got there. Tess was curled up in the gardening section, two customers were browsing, and the whole scene was a leisurely one. Sarah was behind the counter doing not much of anything, which, as far as Louise was concerned, was good. She greeted Louise with a sunny smile but didn't follow her into the back room.

The borrowed folding chairs were already standing in stacks supported by the end of the work table and a full case of books. Was this more assistance from Sarah's young man? She must remember to thank him if it was.

Louise was ready to leave when the phone rang. Sarah picked it up at the counter, then signaled furiously for Louise to come take it.

"It's Ms. Reed," she said in a stage whisper, handing over the phone.

"Viola, how is your aunt?"

"She's doing splendidly, but I'm hoping to be able to remain a few more days. I'll be much more relaxed if I stay until she can get out on her own. Would you mind terribly?"

"Not at all, Viola. That's what friends are for."

"Oh, thank you, Louise. Sarah tells me everything is ready for the book group."

"Yes, and the weather is lovely. We should have a good turnout."

"I do wish I could be there," Viola said wistfully, "but family has to come first."

Louise fully agreed, but she couldn't help being a bit disappointed. She thought Viola might return in time for the meeting because the book group was so important to her.

"I feel on edge about leading the book discussion," she said, voicing her apprehension.

"Oh, you won't have any trouble getting that group to talk," Viola said with a chuckle. "Turning them off may be harder. They're very vocal."

Louise hoped that Viola was right. After she hung up, she surveyed the store with satisfaction. Everything was orderly. Only one thing was missing.

"Did Mr. Trotty come in today?" she asked.

"No, he's resting up for tonight. I told him about the book group, and he's eager to join. This will be his only chance to come to a meeting before he leaves for Ireland."

"He really is going?"

When Louise saw the expression on Sarah's face, she was sorry she'd asked.

"Of course he is, Mrs. Smith! It's something he's wanted to do forever."

"You did a good thing when you convinced him to go."

She was genuinely proud of Sarah for showing concern for the elderly man, but she would still be mightily relieved when Viola returned to take over running the store. At least her helper wasn't hanging the store with fake cobwebs and cardboard ghosts for the meeting.

"Oh, one thing," Sarah said as Louise was ready to leave. "I'm afraid I haven't had a spare minute to read. I haven't even started *A Christmas Carol*. You won't call on me to answer any questions, will you?"

"It's not school," Louise said with an understanding smile. "Your job is to have everything set up before people begin to arrive. I won't be able to get here much before the starting time."

"Oh, you don't need to worry about that. I'll grab a quick bite at the Coffee Shop after the store closes, then come right back here to see that everything is ready. Buck is going to help me."

"I'm sure you'll do fine."

As soon as she was outside the store, Louise was anything but sure. She tried to imagine all the things that might go wrong with Sarah in charge, then felt a bit ashamed of herself for having so little faith in the girl. There was no question that Sarah had good intentions. Fortunately, she didn't have to do anything that was nearly as complicated as the plum pudding.

The day seemed to fly by, maybe because Louise wasn't sure she was ready for the meeting. She'd jotted down a few questions as conversation starters, but what if they weren't enough? What if people just sat there and expected her to say something wise or witty about the book?

In truth, she'd been enthralled when she read it. Tears had clouded her vision when the Cratchit family celebrated Christmas with a dinner that was meager even by Victorian standards but well seasoned by love. She couldn't forget what Tiny Tim said about being in the church. He hoped people saw him so they would remember on Christmas Day "who made lame beggars walk and blind men see."

Perhaps members of the book group had been affected the same way, but would they speak up at the meeting? She could only hope.

When it came time for dinner, she decided to postpone eating. Jane had made a Crock-Pot of vegetable-beef soup that would be just as tasty after the meeting as before it. Louise preferred to spend the little time she had left after her lessons to spruce up.

She chose to wear her navy linen suit and a crisp white blouse with tiny yellow flowers embroidered on the collar. Her silver hair was short but still full, and it fell into place easily after her shower. Still, when she glanced at herself in the mirror, she decided her outfit looked a bit too severe for the meeting. She added her favorite gold earrings set with tiny clusters of blue and amber gemstones, a gift from her dear Eliot on their twentieth wedding anniversary. Her spirits were always buoyed by wearing his present.

The days were getting longer, and she walked to the bookstore before the sun had set. Besides her dark blue clutch purse, she carried her father's copy of *A Christmas Carol* and a few notes she'd made on index cards. It might be nice to read a passage or two aloud if conversation lagged. She tried to think of her favorite part, but the whole tale was such a feast of well-crafted scenes that it was impossible.

A number of people were already in the store when she got there. Mr. Trotty seemed to be the center of attention, perhaps telling about his upcoming trip to Ireland. Florence was there along with several members of Grace Chapel and a few people who were strangers to Louise. She didn't see Sarah, but the girl must have unlocked the store. She had the only key except for the one Viola had given Louise.

Several more people arrived, and Louise had to give Viola credit for generating interest in the classics. The great novels of the past were the book lover's overriding passion, and she certainly had convinced many others to appreciate them, if the turnout was an indication.

Seven o'clock came, but Sarah didn't. Jane and Alice arrived at the last minute, and the young landscaper came with large bakery boxes full of tarts, then left the store. The coffee was brewing in a borrowed machine, and hot water for tea simmered on the hot plate in the back room. There were cups, plates, forks and spoons, all artfully arranged on a table covered by a white linen cloth. Sarah had done everything needed except show up herself. Louise didn't know whether to wait for her or begin the meeting. It went against her nature to start late, but she had an uneasy feeling. The boyfriend had been here, but where could Sarah be?

"If everyone would like to find a seat, I think we'll start now," Louise said, making the decision to begin the meeting. Somewhat to her surprise, they had to bring two chairs from the back room so that everyone had a seat. It was a shame Viola couldn't be there. She would be thrilled by the large turnout.

"I'm Louise Howard," she began, "in case there's anyone here that I haven't met. As most of you know, Viola was called away by a family emergency. I'm pleased to tell you that her aunt came through surgery just fine, and Viola plans to come home on Saturday."

The crowd murmured a bit, but they quickly settled down.

"I think a good place to begin would be—"

The door opened with a familiar tinkle of bells, and Louise was momentarily struck dumb.

With Buck Diesel holding the door open, a tall figure shrouded in a flowing black robe glided into the room extending a thin white hand. Underneath the midnight-black hood, the face of the speaker was masked by a gauzy veil.

"I am the Ghost of Christmas Yet to Come," the creature moaned.

The silver fingernails were a giveaway, of course, but the members of the book group were momentarily stunned.

"Double, double toil and trouble: Fire burn, and caul-dron bubble," the ghostly figure said.

Mr. Trotty laughed.

Did Sarah know she was using the witches' chant from *Macbeth*? Louise remembered Shakespeare's familiar words all these years after reading the play in high school, and apparently others did too. Appreciative laughter became more general as Sarah paraded around the store hunched over with a cardboard sickle that didn't match the role of ghost or witch.

"Thank you, Sarah. You've nicely set the scene for our discussion," Louise said, bringing the ghostly interlude to an end.

Several people clapped, and Sarah dropped the hood and

the gauze covering her face to take a bow, as Louise clenched and unclenched her fingers, and Buck beamed at Sarah, unable to conceal his appreciation for her performance.

"Sarah arranged for our refreshments tonight and set up the chairs and table," Louise said.

From the back of the group, Jane gave her a knowing smile. Louise momentarily wondered whether she should have let Sarah decorate the store with whatever her fertile imagination could concoct, but if Sarah's Grim Reaper costume was any indication, Louise was right to squelch her theatrical talents.

"Now, if we can get on with our discussion," she said, checking her notes to remember what the first question was. "What was your favorite scene in the book?"

"I don't have a favorite scene," Florence said, adjusting her white felt hat, "but what I liked was the way Dickens wrote a really creepy scene, then threw in something funny."

"It's called comic relief," Mr. Trotty said. "Many great writers employed it. It's a break from the intensity of the frightening scenes, but it also serves to magnify the drama of the ones to follow."

Who knew that the man who looked at the same fish book every day could be so astute? Louise certainly never suspected it, but thanks to Sarah, she now knew that he'd only wanted a place to go, a destination beyond the limits of cycling.

"I liked the part where Scrooge saw Marley's ghost but blamed it on something he ate," Jane said.

"I always thought Dickens was maudlin, but now I realize that impression came from seeing a bad movie version of *A Christmas Carol*," a woman said.

"I have to admit I cried in places," Buck said. "The Cratchits were so poor, and Tiny Tim seemed destined to die, the sad little guy."

Louise was momentarily taken aback by the young man's

tender comments but, noticing that Alice had her hand raised, she called upon her sister.

"It's all about the characters," Alice said a bit timidly. "Dickens makes you feel you know them."

"Yes, it's like he paints a picture with words," Mr. Trotty said.

"I even liked Scrooge at the end," Florence said. "When he bought the huge goose, it reminded me of the time I fixed a twenty-two-pound turkey for Christmas, but it snowed so hard that none of my husband's relatives came to eat it."

"I identified with the men who tried to get a donation for the poor from Scrooge," another woman said. "I've solicited for charity, and some people really can be hard-hearted."

"When Scrooge said the poor belonged in workhouses, he was condemning them to a terrible life," Mr. Trotty said. "People had to work like slaves and were barely fed enough to keep them alive. It was a death sentence for many because of disease and malnutrition."

"I guess we don't die of overwork today, but some bosses only care about how much work they can squeeze out of people who work for them," Buck said, speaking up from the back of the room. "Human misery isn't unique to the nineteenth century." His strong shoulders drooped. Then he shook his head slowly and sighed, obviously saddened by the sufferings of the world's workers.

"Everything is different today, but nothing has really changed," a lean man with a weather-beaten face said.

"I guess that's why we're still reading Dickens," Florence offered. "It's like a mirror to us."

Louise hadn't expected such depth of feeling from Buck or such a perceptive comment from Florence, but enthusiasm for Dickens seemed to bring out the best in everyone there. She stepped aside and dropped her note cards in the waste basket behind the checkout counter.

The discussion flowed, and almost everyone joined in.

They'd been talking for over an hour when Louise finally thought to check her watch.

"Friends," she said when there was a momentary lull in the conversation. "Viola gave me one responsibility before we break for refreshments. You need to pick a novel to read for the next meeting."

"I've never read *Moby Dick*," a friend of Viola's from Potterston said.

"You never want to," Florence said. "It's all about hunting whales and boiling blubber. My husband liked it, but I couldn't get through a third of it."

No one came to the defense of Melville's classic, but several other people made suggestions ranging from *Jane Eyre* to *Ivanhoe*.

"I don't know about you folks," Mr. Trotty spoke up, "but I'm going to reread more Dickens, starting with *David Copperfield*. It must be fifty years since I first read it."

"Isn't that an awfully thick book?" Florence asked.

"It's supposed to be his very best book," a Grace Chapel member said.

"He lived a hard life when he was young," Mr. Trotty said. "His sad childhood made the book more personal. I seem to remember that it was his favorite of all the books he wrote."

"Maybe if it's too much to finish by the next meeting, we can read half for that session and the rest for the following meeting," Jane suggested.

Louise looked at her sister with surprise. Jane had just included herself in the group. *A Christmas Carol* must have opened a whole new world for her. She couldn't remember Jane ever spending much time reading classics.

The group embraced Jane's idea enthusiastically, several speaking up in favor of finishing half of the book by the next meeting.

"I found my aunt's old copy of *Alice in Wonderland*," Florence said. "It has really splendid pictures and would be a nice fast read. We could finish it by the next meeting. Why don't we take a vote?"

David Copperfield was the unanimous choice, even Florence reluctantly raised her hand when she saw that she would be the lone holdout.

The group raved over the tarts and finished every one. Some politely complimented Sarah on her dramatic entrance, and others thanked Louise for leading the meeting, although she could honestly say that there had been little for her to do.

Louise looked around for Sarah's boyfriend, hoping to thank him for his insightful comments, but he had slipped away. It was Mr. Trotty who graciously walked Sarah to her car after everyone left and the store was restored to normal.

The three sisters walked home together, enjoying the cool spring breeze and the glow of satisfaction from an evening well spent.

Chapter Fourteen

"Look what I found on the front porch," Louise said, returning to the kitchen with the morning paper and a large manila enevelope. "It has your name on it, Alice."

She handed her sister the envelope with only her first name written on the front.

"That looks like Vera's handwriting," she said, opening the clasp and pulling out a sheath of papers.

"What is it?" Jane asked, busy adding seasonings to a marinade for the chicken breasts she intended to grill for dinner.

"Oh, how sweet!" Alice started spreading papers on the table. "Come look, Jane. They're thank-you notes from Vera's class. You can read them too."

"Here's an artistic soul," Louise said, picking up a sheet of notebook paper with little illustrations all around the edges.

"It's signed *Leslie*," Jane said as she took the paper from Louise for a closer look at the art. "I love children's art. It always seems to come straight from the heart. See how this kitty's tail curls around the stalk of a flower."

"Goodness, I'm not sure who Leslie is. I was so busy chaperoning the boys that I didn't get to know the girls. Maybe she was one of the children who wanted to take an abandoned kitten home on the bus."

"That must have been a memorable moment, finding a litter that had just been left among all those exotic zoo animals," Louise remarked.

"A zoo full of animals from all over the world, and the children got the most excited about some ordinary—but adorable—kittens," Alice said with a laugh.

"Here's a novel one," Jane said. "'Dear Miss Alice Howerd.' He didn't quite get the spelling right."

"What does it say?" Alice was unfolding a rather formal note from Erik.

"'Dear Miss Alice Howerd,'" Jane read. "'You rock. Rocky rocks. It rocks that you shaperont us. Your friend, Chad.'"

"I take it Chad doesn't excel in spelling," Louise said, looking over Jane's shoulder, "but it's the thought that counts."

Alice just smiled at her sister.

"I'd love to read them all, but that will have to wait until later." Jane finished the marinade, put the chicken breasts into the bowl and covered it for the fridge. "I have to get ready to go. Will one of you be here to mind the inn? We have vacancies for the weekend, and someone may call to reserve a room."

"I'm scheduled to work at the hospital at three. There have been so many absences on the staff that I agreed to take time off later," Alice said. "Will you be back before then?"

"I expect so."

"If not, I only have one lesson after school," Louise said. "My pupils try to avoid Friday. I think by the end of the week they're too tired to do their best on the piano."

"Do you want to tell us where you're going?" Alice asked.

"Now that I think about it, you've been a bit distracted all morning." Louise pursed her lips thoughtfully.

"I want to tell you, but I'm not going to." Jane busied herself wiping off the counter.

"Now I'm curious," Alice teased.

"It has to do with Kenneth's decision. If I talk about it, I'm afraid I'll change my mind."

Jane wasn't trying to be secretive with her sisters, but the closer the time came to meet with Rev. Thompson, the more reservations she had. They could easily talk her out of the plan if they didn't think it was a good one. Fortunately, they were both too considerate to pressure her when she preferred to keep something to herself.

She excused herself to go upstairs and get ready. It seemed important to dress with care, not too casual or too formal. Her tailored beige linen jacket and skirt worn with a pale yellow mock turtleneck seemed to fit the bill. She secured her dark hair in a French twist and fastened it with a tortoiseshell comb that had once belonged to her grandmother. Before she left the house, she silently prayed for guidance. It was so hard to know whether she was doing the right thing.

She'd arranged to pick him up at the chapel. He had offered to drive, but she felt more comfortable driving to Potterston in her compact. That way she wouldn't have to give directions or answer questions until they arrived at their destination. She'd invited him on a mystery trip, and that made her the tour guide.

It felt odd to have the tall, lanky minister fold himself into the front seat of her small vehicle. He was dressed in a dark suit and didn't seem to belong in her rather plain car. Or maybe she was feeling so awkward that everything about her plan seemed out of order.

What if he resented her interference? She would hate to lose him as a friend, but she would have to take the risk.

"We couldn't ask for a nicer spring day," he said.

Weather was always a safe topic. Jane commented on her garden, the budding trees and the possibility of rain next week.

"I wish I could get over to finish the chair tomorrow," the

minister said, "but it's spring-cleaning day at the church. I'm afraid I'll be occupied all day."

"Yes, I'll be there for a good portion of the day, too, depending on how many guests we have booked at the inn. I wonder, when you're finished there, could we take another short trip?"

She wasn't looking at his face, but she could sense his surprise.

"Why, I guess so. My sermon is ready for Sunday. Unless there's an emergency, I should be free."

Jane wished there were a church committee to work with their pastor on his potential leave-taking. She was taking so much responsibility into her own hands and, if it backfired, she felt that she would have no one to blame but herself. But until he decided to tell the congregation about his job offer, she had to speak and act for everyone.

The ride to Potterston had never seemed so long. They were expected, but she had no idea how Kenneth would react. Her worst fear was that he would think she was a meddler.

"I'm sorry you couldn't come to the book group," she said. "People made some really good comments. It's amazing how relevant Dickens is after so many years."

"He had an extraordinary grasp of human nature. If I ever find time, I want to reread some of his classics."

Jane knew the streets in Potterston fairly well, although she rarely had any reason to go to the residential area on the east side. The successful merchants, bankers and professional men of the late nineteenth century had built their mansions there, and her destination was one of the most picturesque of the old homes. Many of the big houses were subdivided into apartments or utilized as offices, but they were uniformly well maintained with no commercial signs to detract from the pleasant setting.

She pulled to a stop in front of a solid-looking Redbrick

home. The roof sprouted sharp peaks at irregular intervals with a sturdy brick chimney towering over them all. The shape of the house itself was irregular enough to be endlessly interesting, particularly a corner section with a huge window on the ground floor and a balcony with a double glass-paneled door above it. The railing on the balcony was similar in style to the wrought-iron fence that surrounded the property. The house was flanked by several magnificent oaks, and the landscaping in the yard included many newly planted shrubs, attesting to the care the owner lavished on the grounds.

"It's in the back," Jane said, leaving the car and opening a gate in the fence. She led her companion around to the rear of the house and into an entirely different world.

The spacious backyard had been turned into a children's wonderland with play equipment in all the primary colors. At the moment, no fewer than twenty preschoolers were totally engrossed in games, presided over by three women in yellow smocks. The caregivers had something in common besides their uniform tops. They were all of an age to be retired from such lively employment. Two had silver hair, and the other kept hers an improbable shade of red, immediately reminding Jane of Ethel. They were laughing, seemingly enjoying themselves as much as the children.

Unlike the gate in front, which could be opened by anyone, the entrance to the back had to be unlocked by someone in the yard. It was obvious that none of the children could accomplish it.

The red-haired woman hurried over to let them in, welcoming them with an impish grin.

"Betty told us to watch for you. I take it you're Jane Howard. Your sister Alice was my nurse when I had surgery a few years ago. Such a sweet person! I'm Natalie Foster. This is my sister-in-law, Dottie Foster, and Lillian Henderson. We've drawn playground duty today. It's my favorite job, but the little ones do wear me out sometimes. That's why we switch jobs quite often. None of us is what you would call young."

"This is Rev. Kenneth Thompson," Jane said.

"Just walk right inside that door," Natalie said after the exchange of greetings, indicating a sliding glass door that was obviously a recent addition to the house. "Betty is expecting you."

Jane knew her pastor must be puzzled, but she didn't give him a chance to ask questions. They were met right inside the door by a short, slightly plump woman with a halo of fluffy white hair and a smile that was more welcoming than words could be.

"How nice of you to come, Jane, I'm happy to meet you. I know Kenneth, of course."

To Jane's surprise, she gave the minister a big hug, not easily accomplished because she was a full foot shorter than he was.

"Betty, you're looking well, very well," he said with a wide grin on his face.

"I'll show you the children's area," she said leading the way to a spacious room to the right. "Then I have coffee and a cherry pie waiting in the kitchen. Kenneth, I seem to remember that you have a weakness for tart red cherries."

"You remember well," he said.

"When I converted the house, I allowed one room for play and one for rest time. I put them on opposite sides of the house so there is a quiet place for the little ones who still need two naps."

Jane had never seen a more inviting playroom. It was stocked with every toy imaginable, the smaller ones stored in bright-colored plastic bins. There were small tables and chairs, chalkboards, a sandbox, even a fish tank where goldfish swam in crystal-clear water. In one corner, an assortment of toys with wheels had to be a little boy's dream fleet: a tractor, dump truck, racing car and even a fire engine. A big dollhouse sat in an opposite corner surrounded by strollers, carriages and highchairs filled with a big family of dolls. Jane momentarily felt tempted to examine the well-equipped plastic stove and refrigerator.

"This is a wonderful setup," she said after quietly peeking into a room curtained against the sun, where two babies were asleep in cribs. She marveled that Betty Sagers' day care was even nicer than she'd been told. "But I don't think Kenneth knows exactly what you do here."

"This is an all-volunteer care center for preschoolers," Betty said with justifiable pride. "I have thirty-five people who take turns caring for the children and doing maintenance, most of them retired with time on their hands that they willingly donate. I don't ask anyone to work more than a few hours at a time. Believe me, some days an hour with the children feels like three times that, but I have volunteers who ask for more time than I can give them. Our children all come from low-income families, many with single mothers who couldn't afford to work if they had to pay for regular day care. I mostly get referrals from social-service agencies."

She led them into the kitchen, where two women were preparing sandwiches, cutting them into triangles and arranging them on individual trays. Jane sniffed appreciatively at the aroma of chicken soup. A peek into the pot confirmed that it was homemade.

"I couldn't do this without our lunch ladies," Betty said, introducing them as Gladys and Harriet. "Can you believe, they come every day and make the most wonderful lunches. We rarely have a child who refuses to eat. Of course, we serve breakfast too, because many come to us without eating, but we have another crew for that."

Three pieces of cherry pie with a lattice crust on top were waiting on a tray. Rev. Thompson gave them a longing glance.

"Jane, if you'll carry the pie into the dining room through

that door, I'll bring the coffee. We'll get out of our cooks' way. The children will be famished after their long play session outside. It's been a wonderful morning to be in the yard."

The contrast between the busy, modernized kitchen and the dining room of the stately mansion was breathtaking. They took seats at the end of a mahogany table that was long enough to accommodate twenty. Betty put a silver coffee service in front of her place and poured the beverage into delicate, hand-painted cups edged with gold.

Jane looked around at walls papered with gold brocade and hung with paintings that could rival those of many old masters. The floor was covered by an oriental carpet fine enough to be in a royal dwelling. Through a broad arch, she caught a glimpse of an elegant sitting room with the best of Victorian furniture. She was speechless at the sight of so many beautiful things assembled under one roof, but she wasn't there to be entertained.

"This operation is possible all because of you, Kenneth," Betty said when she sat to join them.

"I couldn't have even imagined a project like this," he said, solemnly shaking his head. "I'm humbled by the number of lives you touch by providing wonderful care for the children."

"Without your grief-counseling center, none of this would have happened. When a friend insisted I go to sessions that you led at the hospital, I was a mess. I didn't think I could go on without my husband after he died."

"You get the credit for your remarkable recovery."

"Kenneth is being tactful," she said to Jane. "I was deeply depressed but too proud to seek help from anyone. I never had children, and I can't possibly tell you how alone I felt. Until I accepted the Lord, I didn't want to go on living."

"You're doing a wonderful thing here," Jane said, trying to hold back her tears.

"I can't begin to tell you how much help I've had. I was

blessed by inheriting this house from my family, and my husband left me more than enough resources to support my plans. Still, without all the volunteers, it couldn't be done. I like to think everyone who helps here takes away something important for their efforts."

She lowered her voice to a whisper. "I believe that my volunteers benefit as much as the children. I know I do. Take Gladys, for example. She's a fantastic cook, but she's also a victim of depression. I met her at grief counseling when she was struggling to reconcile herself to a dear sister's death. We work together to stay positive, and she's every bit as committed to the care center as I am.

"You met Natalie on the playground. She turned her anger against others when her husband left her. Now she's one of my most enthusiastic helpers, and she's seeing a widower socially, the man who helped install the fencing around the playground."

Rev. Thompson shook his head in wonderment. "You're an incredible woman, Betty."

"No, I'm not. Without your counseling program, I probably would have had a sorry end. That's the plain truth, Kenneth. You tossed a stone in the water, and I'm only one ripple of many."

While they enjoyed the refreshments, Betty told them how complicated it had been to get licensed for child care.

"My lawyer came through for me," she said. "In fact, he's so enthusiastic that he doesn't charge for legal work done for the center. I've had good luck with other professionals too. I've arranged free physicals and free dental care with local people. I even got help for an autistic child and counseling for an emotionally disturbed four-year-old. The children are my life, Kenneth, and you made it possible. I'm only sorry that I've been so busy that I haven't kept in touch to let you know how much your grief counseling helped me."

"You've done it all yourself with the Lord's help," he

insisted. "I was aware that you had become involved in some kind of child care, but I never dreamed that you were responsible for something as marvelous as this."

Before they left, he said a prayer for Betty's children, the center, her many helpers and especially for her continued faith in the Lord. Jane was touched by how humble he was about accepting credit for Betty's transformation.

When they left, the children were finishing their lunches. Jane hated to go. She could happily have spent the day getting acquainted with the many energetic little people that Betty had taken under her wing.

"You know, Jane, if you ever have any spare time, we can always use some help with our art program. I've heard from your sister Alice that your talents lie in that direction. Many of us here know her because she's such an outstanding nurse at the Potterston Hospital."

"What kind of help?"

"We need simple projects that our caregivers can master quickly and the children will take pride in doing. At Christmas, for instance, they all make gifts for members of their families. We need ideas, and we wouldn't say no if you were willing to demonstrate a few simple techniques to the children. Some of them are amazingly talented."

"I'll give it serious thought," Jane promised. "I've always been intrigued by children's art. I'll look through my art books and see what could be adapted for preschoolers. Let me try a few things at home and get back to you."

"No hurry," Betty said. "It's a long time until Christmas, although the older I get, the faster time seems to go."

As they walked to her car, Jane thought about the Christmas spirit. She'd always thought it was a December thing, but Charles Dickens and Betty Sagers had given her a different take.

Rev. Thompson was quiet as they headed back to Acorn Hill. She hoped that he would accept the credit that was due him for his grief-counseling program. Certainly he had helped Betty Sagers far more than he had known. She especially liked Betty's description of a stone thrown in the water.

"I know what you're trying to do, Jane," he said at last.

"I hope you don't mind."

"No, you mean well."

Did that mean she hadn't succeeded in swaying him?

"About tomorrow," he said, sounding unusually tentative.

"Spring-cleaning day?"

"That and the other trip you mentioned. Is this a campaign to get me to stay, Jane?"

She badly wanted to deny it, but their friendship was based on honesty.

"It has to do with Dickens."

"Charles Dickens is making you do it?" He raised his eyebrows.

"Well, yes, in a way. You've just met the Ghost of Christmas Past."

He laughed, a loud, spontaneous outburst that encouraged her to say more.

"Tomorrow you'll confront the Ghosts of Christmas Present and Christmas Yet to Come."

He laughed again, and she had an inkling that he might actually enjoy her parade of spirits, whatever her intention.

"I've never seen myself as Scrooge, but I promise not to say, 'Bah! Humbug!' until I've seen all that the specters have in store for me. You do surprise me, Jane."

Was that good or bad? Well, at least he had agreed to see it through to the end.

Chapter 🔔 Fifteen

Jane was grateful when Alice and Louise both came down early Saturday morning to help with breakfast. Four men occupied the four guest rooms, but fortunately they all wanted a 7:00 AM breakfast so they could continue on to an antique car rally in Ohio.

"Who could have predicted that Grace Chapel Inn would become a stopover for club members who restore old cars?" Louise asked as she loaded a tray with sugar, cream, jam and condiments to carry to the dining room.

"Word spreads fast on the Internet," Jane said. "The first group had barely left when last night's reservations came in."

"They've all been so pleasant," Alice said. "We're so fortunate to have such interesting and considerate guests. Several mentioned returning this summer with their wives."

"If you heard much of their conversation, you would say antique autos can become an obsession, but one man mentioned holding rallies for charity and giving rides to terminally ill children," Jane said, checking on the casserole in the oven.

"I guess we're all guilty of getting too wrapped up in our own interests," Louise said. "It was good for me to step outside my comfortable circle of activities and put myself in Viola's place for a while. But I have to admit, I'll be delighted to have her back."

"She'll be here tomorrow for sure?" Alice asked.

"Unless her aunt takes a turn for the worse, and that doesn't seem likely."

Jane was paying only scant attention to her sisters' conversation, but she was immensely grateful to both of them for not bringing up her trip with Rev. Thompson yesterday. She'd told them little, only that they'd visited a woman who had been greatly helped by his grief-counseling program.

"Your oatmeal muffins look luscious," Alice said. "I'm hoping for leftovers."

Jane's buffet had been so well received by their earlier group of auto enthusiasts that she opted to repeat it, only this time she planned ahead. She finished draining bacon on paper towels and set it in the oven to keep warm for a few minutes. She anticipated that this morning's guests would be hearty eaters who wanted a lot of protein to begin the day.

"I thought I would go to the chapel and help with spring cleaning," Alice said.

"I'm going over first thing, but I'll have to leave around noon to check on Sarah at the store," Louise said. "I enjoy the group effort to spruce things up. The church always looks so nice when the work is done. Are you going, Jane?"

"Yes, as soon as things are under control here."

She'd lain awake last night trying to imagine how the day would go. Rev. Thompson had been a good sport about the Ghost of Christmas Past, but today could she expect a similar reaction?

The guests came down in a whirlwind of high spirits and made quick work of her bountiful buffet. After they left, her sisters enjoyed the muffins Jane had saved for them, but she had no appetite herself. She nibbled on half a muffin to avoid stirring the maternal instincts of her sisters.

"Is that all you're going to have?" Alice asked when Jane abandoned her meager meal and began cleaning up.

"I'm not very hungry this morning."

Alice accepted her answer without comment, and Jane had an urge to hug her. Her sisters had a gift for giving her space when she needed it. Perhaps that was why the three of them worked so well together.

In spite of her planning, she wasn't able to leave the inn until after nine o'clock. Alice insisted on helping with the cleanup, and she was in the mood to chat. Jane didn't want to shoo her away, but she hoped to get to the chapel before nine, the time scheduled to begin work.

Jane was dressed for work in jeans and an orange corduroy shirt. Ordinarily, she would have opted to work outside. There were shrubs to trim, flower beds to plant and a great deal of sweeping in the parking area. She'd noticed that the trim around the back door needed some touch-up paint, and there were probably dozens of other jobs to do on the exterior of the building. Today, however, she wanted to be inside where her pastor would be working.

Grace Chapel was a lovely white clapboard church built in the late nineteenth century, and the congregation went to great pains to maintain it as a fitting monument to their faith. A building over a hundred years old did require a great deal of loving care, and it was fortunate to have a congregation that wholeheartedly supported the effort. If today went the way of most spring cleanings, volunteers for every task would be at work.

Jane had watched her father roll up his sleeves and spearhead the repairs and cleaning of the chapel, teaching by example as much as through his preaching. Rev. Thompson did the same. He never asked a member of the congregation to do something he wouldn't do himself, even when it meant standing on the very top of a tall ladder to capture cobwebs on the ceiling.

She'd hoped for a quiet moment with him before people came in force, but the street was lined with cars by the time she got there.

Florence's husband, Ronald Simpson, was chairman of the building and grounds committee this year and, as such, he was in charge of spring cleaning. He was a quiet, unassuming man in his seventies, usually seen with a pipe—lit or unlit—clenched between his teeth. He tolerated his wife's excess of enthusiasm with good humor and was a natural leader when it came to projects like keeping the chapel in top condition.

Jane knew she should report to him for her first assignment, but she needed the reassurance of seeing her pastor ahead. She went in through the double doors in front because most of the activity seemed to be centered in the back, where Ronald was holding a clipboard and talking to several people.

"Jane, I'm so glad you're here."

Florence came down the aisle dressed as though she planned to deal with hazardous waste. She wore heavy blue rubber gloves, and she'd stuffed herself into a pair of off-white canvas trousers, over which she wore a smock. Her hair was completely covered by a white turban that could have been the remains of an old sheet. No question, Florence was there to do battle with every dust mite and germ that could have invaded the chapel. First, though, Florence wanted to rally her troops.

"I know you're a whiz with plants and gardening, Jane, but before Ronald gives you a job, I was hoping you would inspect the pews and see if there's any damage to repair. You have such a good eye for scratches and such."

Jane knew exactly what Florence had in mind, because she went through this ritual every year on cleaning day. She wanted Jane to examine every pew for blemishes that could be polished away or touched up with a stain stick. No matter how carefully Jane checked each and every one, Florence would follow behind her and point out minute scratches, lecturing her about the importance of "a stitch in time."

"I can't right now, Florence. I have to see Kenneth."

She escaped, a bit proud of herself for standing up to Florence. No doubt the woman would recruit others to follow her orders. In spite of her overbearing ways, she was respected for the sheer volume of work she accomplished for the church.

Jane hurried down to the lower level, hoping to catch her pastor alone for a moment. Instead, she caught him on the run, just about to go out the door.

"Kenneth, do you have a minute?"

"Not now, I'm afraid. I have to get to the hospital."

Her first reaction was that something was wrong with him, but, of course, a minister was always on call for emergencies.

"I'm going with you."

He looked surprised but didn't object. She followed in his wake as he said a few quick words to Ronald and ran toward his car. He had the engine running before she got in beside him and quickly fastened her seat belt.

"What's wrong?" she asked, feeling a little breathless from keeping up with him.

"I got a call that Mr. Trotty has been rushed to the hospital in Potterston with a possible heart attack."

"Oh, that poor man. Just when he was planning the trip of a lifetime. I didn't know he was a member of Grace Chapel, though. I'm surprised anyone called you."

"Actually, he was baptized there a long time ago, but he hasn't been active since he returned to Acorn Hill after his retirement."

"I believe you would respond to anyone who asked for your help, even if you'd never seen him before," Jane said thoughtfully.

"Is that the Ghost of Christmas Present speaking?" he asked with a faint smile.

"Perhaps, but it's true. I doubt you've ever turned down a request for help."

"Don't make me out to be a saint, Jane. That way I won't disappoint you."

She didn't know how to answer, and they rode with little conversation the rest of the way to the hospital in Potterston. Whatever she'd expected when they got there, it wasn't the startling presence of Sarah Lister, who hovered in the emergency waiting room.

"Sarah, what's wrong?" Her first instinct was that the young woman had hurt herself.

"Oh, I'm so glad to see you, Jane. Rev. Thompson, I've never experienced anything like this, and I really need help."

"What is your problem, Sarah?" he asked.

Jane didn't see any sign of injury. In fact, Sarah seemed to be wholly intact, but she did seem to be greatly agitated.

"Oh, the problem isn't mine. Mr. Trotty came into the store earlier than usual, but he didn't seem to be his usual chipper self—well, not chipper exactly, but he's been happier since he's signed up for his trip."

"What's wrong with Mr. Trotty, Sarah?" Rev. Thompson asked in the kindest possible voice.

"I was afraid he was having a heart attack. He didn't want to come here, but I insisted."

"Mr. Trotty was having heart pains, and you drove him here." The minister had been present for the great pot-holder fire. He seemed to understand Sarah-speak.

"Yes. Now no one will tell me anything, but you're a minister. They have to let you see him, don't they?"

"It depends on the situation. I can't interfere if he's receiving treatment. Let me talk to the nurse on duty and see what I can find out."

"If he dies, it will be all my fault," Sarah wailed, turning to Jane after Rev. Thompson left.

"No, it certainly will not," Jane said firmly.

"But I got him all excited about the trip. Maybe it was too much for his heart. He's terribly old, you know."

"Whatever is wrong with him, it's not your fault," Jane said insistently. "Happiness didn't give him a heart attack."

Sarah wasn't convinced. She paced from one end of the

waiting area to the other, managing to stumble over a pair of crutches belonging to the only other patient in the room, but she regained her balance without falling.

Jane was worried too. It would be a terrible shame if Mr. Trotty couldn't go on the trip he'd always wanted to take. She forgot about spring cleaning at the chapel and fervently wished Rev. Thompson would come back with some news.

Sarah finally sat down beside Jane. She made little whimpering sounds and continued to blame herself for Mr. Trotty's heart pains. Jane wasn't able to say anything that comforted her. She wished Alice were here. Her sister was an expert at knowing how to handle situations like this.

They waited less than thirty minutes, but it seemed much longer before the pastor came out of the door that led to emergency care. Much to her surprise—and happiness—Mr. Trotty walked out beside him.

"Mr. Trotty! Are you all right?" Sarah cried out.

She rushed forward so exuberantly that Jane was afraid she would topple the little man.

"It seems," Rev. Thompson said, answering for Mr. Trotty, "that kippered herring in sour cream isn't the most appropriate breakfast for a senior citizen."

"I would have been all right if I'd cooked the onions longer. Never could tolerate raw onions."

"Not a heart attack?" Sarah said incredulously.

"Heartburn," the pastor said, "but it turned out all right. It gave me a chance to get acquainted with Henry. You did the right thing to drive him here, Sarah. That took great presence of mind."

Sarah radiated pleasure at the minister's compliment.

"They gave me a prescription for some gas medicine," Mr. Trotty said, sounding a bit put out about it. "I guess it won't hurt to take some with me to Ireland so I can eat whatever I want."

Rev. Thompson shook hands with Mr. Trotty, and Jane

gave both him and Sarah a hug. The Ghost of Christmas Present couldn't have planned a better way to show the minister how much people in the community relied on him. She would have to think of a subtle way to mention it on the way back to the chapel. Rev. Thompson thought he wasn't doing a special job in carrying out his mission as pastor of Grace Chapel? His parishioners would undoubtedly declare, "Bah! Humbug!" to that!

They reached the pastor's car when a sudden thought hit Jane. She looked around and saw Sarah and Mr. Trotty in the next row of cars.

"Sarah!" she called out with urgency.

"What's wrong?" She walked back toward Jane.

"What about the bookstore?"

Sarah looked stunned.

"Oh no!"

"Did you lock up for the morning?"

Sarah slowly shook her head.

"Did you get someone to watch it?"

She continued shaking her head as though in a trance.

"You just walked out?"

"I was so scared about Mr. Trotty that I never thought. Mrs. Smith is going to hate me."

"You did what needed to be done, Sarah," Rev. Thompson said. "I'm sure Mrs. Smith will understand."

"She will," Jane wearily agreed, thinking to herself that Louise would be the happiest person in town when Viola got home.

❀

Louise was pleased by the turnout for spring cleaning. There were so many people that it took her a few minutes to find a job. She opted to check the hymnals in the racks on the back of the pews, removing old bulletins, Sunday school papers and other miscellaneous items that had been stuck inside.

She pulled two that were badly in need of repair, wondering if it would be better to have them rebound or replaced.

That done, she applied herself to straightening the music used by the choir. She thought of herself as a born organizer, and there were always things that got out of place when they were used by a number of people. Fortunately, her self-appointed jobs kept her out of Florence's way. She wouldn't mind dusting, polishing or scrubbing; she just didn't want to do it with Florence looking over her shoulder. She seemed especially officious this year, probably because her husband was in charge of the workday.

Louise found it immensely satisfying to see how many people cared about the chapel. She was in such a mellow mood that she stepped forward to polish the piano used for choir rehearsals when Florence asked for a volunteer. Louise had to give her credit. Florence liked to tell others what to do, but she worked hard herself. Her turban was lopsided, and both trouser knees were dark with dust where she'd been kneeling to reach into corners.

Time flew, and Louise was beginning to wonder where Jane was. She carried an armload of empty cartons that had once held candles to be hauled away with the other trash, and there was no sign of Jane in the kitchen or outside, the places where her sister would most likely be working.

Alice was industriously cleaning the refrigerator along with another woman when Louise stopped in the kitchen for a cup of tea.

"Jane is keeping herself scarce," Alice said. "I wonder where she is. She planned to make a day of it."

Someone was running a rather noisy floor polisher in the Assembly Room, so it took a minute to realize that someone else was shouting.

They both hurried to see what was happening and discovered that the loud protests were coming from one of the sweetest women in the congregation. Mary Linz was so mild mannered and pleasant that it was hard to believe she was actually yelling. In fact, she was so furious that Florence could only stand there with her mouth open and no words coming out.

"I dusted the pews, which didn't even need it. You followed behind me and did them over. I changed the altar cloth, and you straightened it. I polished glass, and it was too smudged for you. I ran the vacuum, and you accused me of not changing the bag before I started. I quit! I have half a mind to quit the chapel. You are the most impossible person I've ever met. I will never, ever work on anything with you again."

"If you weren't so careless, I wouldn't have to do things over," Florence said, her voice a weak imitation of her usual one.

Louise didn't know whether to intervene or to ignore the altercation. Alice's distress showed on her face. She hated discord, and such a fierce argument at Grace Chapel would bother her for days.

"What seems to be the matter?"

Louise hadn't seen Rev. Thompson come into the Assembly Room, but she was immensely relieved that he was there.

"Mary, Florence, is there something I can help with?"

Louise caught a glimpse of Jane hovering in the background. When she tactfully went back outside, it was a clue for both Louise and Alice to return to the kitchen. Their pastor was here now. He would know what to do.

⟲⟳

Fifteen minutes later, Jane returned to the Assembly Room and found Florence and Mary working side by side, washing down the folding tables that were set up for meetings and special events. Mary said something, and Florence laughed. Rev. Thompson had calmed the stormy waters. Jane marveled at the tact and understanding that he brought to their congregation.

Gradually, the workers began to leave. The church literally sparkled, and Jane couldn't have done a better job with the landscaping if she'd spent days working on it herself. Rev. Thompson thanked each volunteer and gave an especially heartfelt thank-you to Ronald and Florence.

Jane finished cleaning up the sandwich luncheon that had been provided for the workers and went to Rev. Thompson's office, hoping that he remembered his promise to go on one more trip with her.

"Ah, it's the Ghost of Christmas Present," he teased when he saw her.

"I hope you saw yourself as I saw you today," she said thoughtfully.

"Jane." He sounded weary.

She was tempted to leave him in peace, but more was at stake than just what she wanted.

"How can the Ghost of Christmas Present not point out how much you mean to so many people? You rushed to the hospital even though Mr. Trotty isn't an active member of the church. It says a lot that Sarah felt she could call on you. You've become an integral part of the community. If you leave, there will be a huge spiritual void."

"I think you're exaggerating. You mean well, Jane, but I only do what any minister would do."

"What about Mary? Florence could easily have bullied her into quitting the chapel."

"It was only a momentary reaction on Mary's part."

"You're one of the few people that Florence truly respects. You averted a crisis. I don't know what you said to them, but it must have come from your heart."

"I only suggested that we pray together for a few moments. The Lord's peace is very calming."

"What will you be doing if you take the new job?" Jane asked bluntly.

"I'll be setting up interviews, arranging for speakers and generally overseeing several programs on the church station."

"Is that really what you want to do? I wouldn't oppose it if you wanted to move to a larger church with greater challenges, but that doesn't sound like a job that requires a minister."

"You may be right, but I really haven't made up my mind." He sounded as dejected as she'd ever heard him.

"I'm going to hold you to your promise. You know, to come with me one more time."

"Believe it or not, I'm curious to meet the Ghost of Christmas Yet to Come. I found my old copy of *A Christmas Carol* and read it until the wee hours last night. This time I'll drive, though."

Didn't he like her driving? Or did he feel too cramped in her small car? Jane opened her mouth to ask, then decided it was unimportant. She had to learn to pick her issues wisely. She followed him out to his car.

Peckford wasn't a ghost town, but it was as close to being one as any in their county. She'd written down the directions from an old school friend, Laura. As kids, they'd sat around campfires at church camp telling ghost stories about Peckford. Laura's grandmother lived alone in a spooky house on the main street, and once Laura took Jane with her on a visit. The house had closets large enough to hide a dozen kids, and beds with carved headboards that went up to the ceiling. It also had a secret passage that led from behind a bookcase in the parlor to the basement. The grandmother took great pride in telling that her family once concealed runaway slaves, but her own granddaughter was skeptical.

It took longer than Jane expected to get to the town, and she began to feel guilty for taking up so much of the pastor's time. Saturday was supposed to be his day of rest so he would be fresh for the Sunday service, but he'd spent it at the church and hospital. He looked a bit weary.

The sun was low, but it was still daylight when they got to Peckford. She was glad not to arrive there in the dark. The town was singularly uninviting. Half the stores on Main Street were boarded up, and there was an air of decay and neglect everywhere. Laura's grandmother had passed on, and for a while the house was taken over by squatters. At last the family paid to have it torn down, fearing lawsuits if someone was injured on the site. There was never any question of selling it. There was no market for houses in Peckford, nor was there any shortage of clapboard houses with the paint worn away. Even the best houses, huge brick buildings weighed down by ivy left to the effects of time, had a sad, neglected look.

"Keep going," Jane directed, knowing the way by heart now. "After you cross a bridge, take the first right."

If her companion was curious, he kept silent. Jane only vaguely remembered being here with her friend when they were both around twelve. There was a poorly tended cemetery on the left, and then they came to their destination.

The church had been built of granite to last for centuries, and for the first hundred years it had been a bastion of faith, a place where people came in times of joy and sorrow to give thanks to the Lord and receive the consolation of faith.

"Stop here." Jane sounded a little hoarse.

She got out of the car, and Kenneth followed. The church windows had been boarded up long enough for the wood to turn a weathered gray. Graffiti marred the stone walls, and the front door hung open on rusty hinges.

Rev. Thompson didn't say anything. Jane didn't need to. The message was clear. The house of worship was an abandoned ruin.

They cautiously entered through the unsecured door, taking care where they stepped. With the windows boarded up, it was difficult to see more than outlines where the pews had been removed and carted away. At the front, there was no sign of an altar. The air reeked of mice, mildew and decay. Jane was dismayed at the condition of the old church.

"They lost their minister, and no other wanted to come to such a small, impoverished town. Gradually, everyone moved away except for a few diehards and those too elderly to begin again elsewhere," she said, finding her voice after several awkward minutes of exploring.

"You play hardball, Ghost of Christmas Yet to Come." Rev. Thompson made a little noise that was somewhere between a sigh and a laugh.

Jane left the church without him. It seemed a long time before he joined her.

Chapter  Sixteen

Jane worked late into the night until her eyes were blurry and her back ached from bending over the rocker. Fortunately, she had already cleaned the wood with steel wool and lacquer thinner in preparation for the varnish that Rev. Thompson had purchased and left in the shed.

The antique oak was in surprisingly good condition once the blushing—a whitish haze—had been worked off, and it didn't seem to require any staining. She didn't know if the pastor expected her to complete the work, but she wanted him to have a finished chair to take with him if he decided to leave.

She had doubts that he would stay.

The chair would still be tacky tomorrow, but by Monday it would be dry enough to move. The light in the shed left something to be desired, so she used a powerful flashlight to check the surface for missed spots. When she was satisfied that the wood had an even coat, she stood and began cleaning the brush and straightening up the shed.

Tomorrow she would take a few minutes to condition the leather seat with a special oil made for that purpose, and by Monday she should be able to lightly sand the wood and apply a coat of wax to it. It was a beautifully crafted chair, whomever the maker, and she hoped her work lived up to her friend's expectations.

After the cleanup for breakfast Sunday morning, Jane went about setting out an array of food on the buffet in the dining room. To add variety, she'd refrigerated a gelatin mold using fresh cherries, cranberry juice and orange pieces. It would provide color and go well with the rest of her preparations. She was checking to be sure everything was in place when Alice came into the dining room.

"I was just about to go upstairs to get ready for church," Jane said.

"Did you want to wait to set out the salt and pepper?" Alice tactfully asked, noticing that they were missing.

"Oh dear, I'm getting forgetful. I'll fetch them."

"No, let me. I'm ready to go." Alice smoothed the skirt of her moss-green linen suit and smiled at her sister. "You look tired. Did you sleep poorly?"

"No, just not long enough. I worked on Kenneth's rocker last night."

"Whatever for?"

"I just wanted it to be in good shape if he decides to leave."

"We don't know that he will," Alice said, ever the optimist. "Even if he does, he'll give the chapel adequate notice. You didn't need to lose sleep over a chair."

"I know," Jane said, feeling a bit impatient but attributing it to her lack of sleep. "It was just something I wanted to do."

Alice wisely said nothing more, and Jane hurried upstairs to dress for church.

She slipped into a long-sleeved brown dress with a small white collar that always made her feel like a Pilgrim. Her clunky-heeled leather shoes contributed to the somber aspect of the dress, and she couldn't remember why she'd bought it. At least it matched her mood today.

Alice had told Louise about Jane's late-night work on the rocker. It was Jane's way of dealing with anxiety, and maybe it was a good one. Louise had tried not to dwell on the possibility of Rev. Thompson's leaving, but she was terribly concerned.

Jane had explained the nature of the job he was considering. It seemed like a waste of his talent for working with people, but Louise thought she knew that sometimes the Lord led in unexpected directions. Perhaps it was only a prelude to something else.

Or maybe Rev. Thompson needed the change to renew his enthusiasm. She knew from her father's experience that sometimes the Lord laid a heavy burden on His servants. Not everyone who was called showed the strength to carry through.

When the sermon began, she decided to make a special effort to listen for any clue their pastor might give about his intentions. She could see Jane staring ahead intently and realized that her sister was doing the same. Would he announce his departure this morning? Jane said he had to make his decision by tomorrow. If he was planning to leave, surely this was his best opportunity to explain his reasons to the congregation.

Much as she hated to admit it, the sermon wasn't up to his usual inspirational power.

"'You are the salt of the earth,'" he began, reading from Matthew 5:13. "'But if the salt loses its saltiness, how can it be made salty again? It is no longer good for anything, except to be thrown out and trampled by men.'"

This passage had always seemed a bit obscure to Louise. She never felt that she fully understood it. Did Jesus mean that salt was like faith, once lost it couldn't be regained? That thought confused her even more.

Was there a personal message in what the pastor was saying? She didn't think so, but she acknowledged that it must be exceedingly difficult to prepare a fresh, inspirational sermon every Sunday. Maybe he needed the stimulation of a new position in a new place to inspire his best work for the Lord.

Her father always knew when one of his sermons wasn't effective: The congregation would be restless, coughing and shifting positions. Although he always prepared carefully, he accepted that sometimes he would fall short of expectations. It was the nature of preaching. Most often he hit a responsive chord, but there were times when his listeners couldn't follow his theme.

The pastor talked a bit about the importance of salt in the ancient world, how it was sometimes used to pay Roman soldiers. The modern word *salary* came from the Latin word for salt.

Louise's mind wandered, despite her earlier determination not to let that happen. She was taken by surprise when the sermon ended, and she realized that she'd missed the point, whatever it was.

"He didn't say a word about his plans," Jane whispered to her. "I thought for sure he would."

After the service, she slipped away from Louise and Alice, making her way home through the rear entrance instead of going out the front, where the pastor was greeting the congregation in the fresh air of a beautiful spring day.

Louise didn't blame her. Jane had told them enough about her Christmas ghost idea for her sister to understand that she was slightly embarrassed by it. She'd tried to give the minister reasons to stay. If she'd failed, she was going to feel like a meddler, a role totally alien to Jane's nature.

Jane got home ahead of them and set out the remaining food for their meal. When the sisters were seated and the blessing said, their talk turned to the morning service.

"I didn't understand Kenneth's sermon," Louise admitted. "Although I have to confess that I wasn't paying very close attention."

"I'm glad you said that. I kept trying to find a hidden message in what he was saying, so I didn't really follow his theme. I was hoping he would approach the congregation before he speaks to the people who want to hire him."

"Maybe he's decided to stay."

Jane shook her head sadly. "If he had, I think he would have let me know."

Louise knew she was right. Rev. Thompson was the kindest person she knew. He wouldn't leave Jane in suspense after all she'd done to convince him to stay.

"You look exhausted," she said to Jane. "Why don't you take a nap? I'll clean up and do the dishes."

"You know, I think that's a good idea."

No protest? No urgent job that had to be done first? Louise was amazed that Jane so readily agreed to her suggestion, but it only increased her concern. They would all miss their pastor if he left, but Jane would take it as a personal failure. He'd been her mentor, guiding her to renewed faith. She'd tried to reciprocate by letting him know how important he was to the church and the community.

Louise watched her leave. Jane's shoulders sagged with disappointment, and her steps lacked spring as she went toward the stairs.

～∞

Jane couldn't believe that she'd slept nearly three hours. Goodness! Even as a baby, she'd been a poor nap taker. She couldn't remember the last time she'd slept into the afternoon.

She came downstairs to a happy scene.

"Here's Jane," Louise said, sounding delighted. "Jane, Viola is back!"

"Welcome home. I was so happy to hear that your aunt came through her surgery so well," Jane said.

"I was glad to be there for her, but you don't know how pleased I am to be home. Thankfully, Sarah did well at the store, according to what you've told me. I would never have left her in charge without you to look after her, Louise. I can't possibly tell you how grateful I am. Oh, I've brought you all a gift."

She handed over a heavy plastic bag.

"Fresh shrimp. They're packed well to stay frozen, and they've been shelled and cleaned, but you'll want to do something with them fairly soon. They're nice jumbo size, not the little ones that sometimes don't seem worth the effort they require. There's a market near my aunt's house, and I couldn't resist bringing some back to you."

"That's very thoughtful," Alice said, taking them from her. "Thank you."

Jane relieved her sister of the heavy package and had an idea.

"Come back this evening, Viola. We'll feast on shrimp jambalaya to celebrate your return."

"Oh, I couldn't ask you to cook for me," Viola protested. "I meant the shrimp as a gift for you to enjoy."

"There's nothing we enjoy more than sharing a meal with a friend," Louise assured her.

"Well, if you're sure, I'd love to. Now I have to get home and see how my cats are doing. If they missed me half as much as I missed them, we'll have quite a reunion. Oh, did Sarah do everything necessary to get ready for the book group?"

All three sisters were silent for a moment. Then Louise spoke for all of them.

"She did just fine. We think she's a delightful girl, a bit flighty at times, but she did some good things while you were gone."

"She convinced Mr. Trotty to take a trip to Ireland," Alice said.

"And she took him to the emergency room when he was having chest pains. Nothing serious, fortunately, but she acted with great presence of mind," Jane said.

"Really? My Sarah?" Viola looked astonished.

"I have an idea," Jane said. "Let's ask Sarah to join us tonight. Tell her she can bring her gentleman friend."

"I'll call and ask her," Viola volunteered. "I want to thank her for coming through for me. And I want to hear all about the book group."

"It was a smashing success. They're going to read *David Copperfield*, half for next time and the other half for the meeting after that," Louise said.

"Wonderful!" Viola beamed her approval. "I'll see you later then."

"Why don't you come around seven?" Jane said, glad to have dinner preparations to keep her focused.

Viola left, her high-heeled shoes clacking on the floor of the entryway. She turned around, tossed the end of her long orange and rose scarf over her shoulder and smiled broadly. "It is so good to be home!"

After Viola left and her sisters scattered, Jane took the frozen shrimp to the kitchen. She was genuinely pleased by Viola's gift. She could tolerate the work involved in preparing shrimp because the results were so luscious.

Her first job was to separate the frozen shrimp before she boiled them. She ran cold water over them while she waited for the water in her big canning kettle to heat. To help bring out the flavor and cut down on the fishy smell, she added several celery sticks and lemon wedges to the boiling water, then immersed the shrimp.

It was important to stay close to the stove to watch them. The shrimp would cook quickly, even after she turned the heat down for a gentle boil. She would know they were done when they turned a pleasing shade of pink.

Her jambalaya recipe called for two pounds of cooked shrimp. Viola had given her at least three pounds raw. She adjusted her recipe accordingly, realizing that she could feed several more people. While she ran cold water over the cooked shrimp, she phoned Ethel to see if she wanted to join them.

"Oh, you should have asked me sooner," her aunt lamented. "I've already promised to go to dinner and a movie with a friend."

Jane hoped the guests who were coming had hearty appetites.

When the shrimp were cool enough to handle, she placed them in a large bowl. They were exceptionally big and meaty. The jambalaya was going to be spectacular, a chef's dream presentation.

∞

Shortly before seven, Jane was ready for dinner guests. A great pot of rice was steaming on a back burner, and the Cajun sauce was simmering, waiting for the last-minute addition of parsley and shrimp. Jane's recipe called for canned tomatoes. Those, along with diced bacon, chopped green pepper, onions and celery, combined with garlic and an array of seasonings to produce the exotic aroma that filled her kitchen.

Because the main course was so rich, she decided to keep the rest of the meal simple. She served a variety of warmed rolls to accompany the jambalaya. For anyone who would have room for dessert, she had ambrosia chilling in the fridge.

She heard the front door open and went out to welcome Viola, who looked festive in a long, royal blue skirt, a gold silk blouse and her signature scarf in shades of emerald, gold and blue.

"I feel guilty, coming to eat the gift I gave you," she said.

"It's the best possible kind of gift—one that can be shared," Louise said, coming from the parlor, where she'd been practicing a piece on the piano.

"Sarah will be coming later," Viola said. "I do hope she's on time. Your jambalaya smells heavenly. I wouldn't want it to overcook while we wait for her."

"It can't," Jane assured her. "The shrimp don't go in until the last few minutes. The longer the sauce simmers, the better it will taste."

There was a rap on the door, and Alice came down the stairs just in time to answer it.

"I hope we're not too late," Sarah said, taking care to lift a corner of her long floral skirt as she stepped into the inn.

All heads turned in her direction.

"I'm so glad you allowed me to invite Mr. Trotty."

"I thought . . ." Viola began.

"I know, that I would ask Landscaping Dude. He's history. He has a kind heart, but can you imagine—he spends every weekend in the summer racing dirt bikes? His idea of a hot date is me watching him ride. Dust, mud, smelly motors. Yuck!"

"We're awfully glad you came, Mr. Trotty," Louise said.

"We most certainly are," Jane said with a gracious smile.

"And I'm most grateful for your kind invitation." Mr. Trotty gave a gentle bow of his head.

"Don't worry! Henry promised to take his pill. No more heartburn!" Sarah said.

"Good. Everyone, just have a seat in the parlor. We can eat in a few minutes." Jane left to check on dinner.

Alice shepherded their guests, and Louise followed Jane into the kitchen.

"Tell me what I can do," Louise said.

"Put ice in the glasses and pour the water," Jane said. "And see if you can reach the big serving tureen on the top shelf over the fridge."

"It seems our Sarah is full of surprises," Louise said. "She confessed to me earlier that she never knew either of her grandfathers. It's a new experience for her to get to know a man as old as Mr. Trotty."

"Landscaping Dude didn't last long, did he?" Jane said with a laugh. "I thought he was a nice fellow. He certainly helped out with the book group."

Louise gave an exaggerated sigh. "Ah, the ways of love are hard to figure."

Jane was satisfied with the succulent shrimp dish on her

stove. Now she only needed to serve it up. She was about to do just that when she heard a familiar voice in the entryway.

"Jane, anyone home?"

"Kenneth," she said under her breath.

She went out to greet him, wondering what his visit might signify.

"If my nose doesn't deceive me, I've come at an inconvenient time," he said.

"You've come at the perfect time. I'm about to serve shrimp jambalaya. Viola brought the shrimp back from her trip, and I've made enough to serve a dozen people. Please tell me you'll join us."

"I couldn't impose."

"You haven't had dinner, have you?"

"No, but—"

"Then I won't take no for an answer."

"First I have to tell you—"

"Come into the kitchen." She noticed that Louise had made herself scarce. "After dinner, I want to show you the rocker. I hope you don't mind that I've just about finished it."

"Mind? I'm delighted." He shuffled his feet and grinned boyishly. "I don't know when I've smelled anything so delicious. You must have other guests to have made so much."

"Viola is here, and Sarah came with Mr. Trotty."

"I'll be pleased to stay, but I didn't come here to eat, Jane."

"No, I didn't think you had."

She busied herself unnecessarily to avoid looking directly at him. If he gave her bad news, she wanted a moment to compose herself.

"First let me say, I found it immensely illuminating to talk to Rev. Granger. He sent me a letter after our dinner, mentioning among other things how your father had steered him through some confusing times in his life and ministry. If you'd done nothing else for me, I would be very grateful for the opportunity to have met him."

"I'm glad," Jane said. "My father held him in high esteem for his commitment to the Lord."

"I was overwhelmed by your take on the Ghosts of Christmas Past, Present and Yet to Come," Rev. Thompson continued. "You put yourself to so much trouble on my behalf that I hardly have words to express my gratitude."

"Don't thank me. I did it selfishly. I couldn't bear the thought of the chapel without you as our minister. I wasn't thinking of what was best for you."

"I don't for one minute believe that. So much of your early life is vested in the chapel and your father's role there that you just wanted to keep things as they are."

"We have to be able to accept change. I should have learned that by now." She stirred the jambalaya, but she was so intent on her friend's words that she barely saw it.

"I'm staying."

"What?" She swung around, afraid to believe his words.

"You were right. I'm not destined for the business of producing radio shows. I don't know if I'm wholly adequate for the needs of the congregation, but with the Lord's help, I'll continue to try. After all, as the wise poet John Milton once wrote, 'They also serve who only stand and wait.'"

She blinked back tears of happiness.

"I didn't mean to keep you in suspense. It was a very difficult decision."

"Yes, I'm sure it was. Goodness, perhaps I've put too much spice in the sauce. It's making my eyes water. Would you mind going to the parlor and bringing everyone to the dining room for dinner?"

"My pleasure, but first I want you to be certain of how much I appreciate everything you did for me. I don't know what my decision would have been without your guidance."

"If God was using me, all credit goes to Him. Now please go to the parlor. If I don't find a tissue, I'm going to blubber."

He laughed, and she found it impossible not to smile.

"You can be the one to tell your sisters."

"At dinner?"

"Anywhere you like."

Jane didn't know when a dinner had ever seemed so special. Rev. Thompson said a heartfelt blessing, everyone raved about the jambalaya, and Jane felt a great weight lift from her shoulders.

"This is a triple celebration," she said. "First to welcome Viola home, then to wish Mr. Trotty a trip that will enable him to realize his dreams."

Their friends applauded Viola and Sarah's escort.

"And the third?" Louise asked.

"Rev. Thompson has decided . . . not to accept his job offer. He'll be staying at Grace Chapel. I'm so thankful to him and to the Lord that I can hardly speak."

"I owe a debt of gratitude to those who helped me make my decision, especially Rev. Granger, an old friend of Rev. Daniel Howard, and the Ghosts of Christmas Past, Present and Yet to Come. Thank you, Jane."

There was explaining to do, because only the Howard sisters had known about the possibility of the minister's leaving or Jane's three ghosts.

Mr. Trotty thanked his new friends and expressed special gratitude to Sarah.

"I'm celebrating too," Sarah said when the conversation died down. "I have a new career now that Ms. Reed doesn't need me anymore."

Everyone in the room held in a breath.

"I'm going to be a tour guide. They have these buses that take people all over the country, mostly older people who don't drive anymore. My first assignment will be Tulip Time in Holland, Michigan. There will be six million tulips in bloom in May. Isn't that splendid? I can hardly wait."

Jane smiled and congratulated her, as did everyone else in the room, but she couldn't help imagining Sarah hunting for lost seniors in endless fields of bright-colored blooms.

Moussaka via Nia
SERVES EIGHT

⚭

2 eggplants, peeled and sliced
2 large potatoes, peeled and thinly sliced

MEAT SAUCE

1 pound ground lamb or chuck
2 medium onions, thinly sliced
1 26-ounce can tomato sauce
1 teaspoon dried basil
½ teaspoon oregano or thyme
1 teaspoon salt
2 crushed garlic cloves
½ teaspoon cinnamon
¼ teaspoon pepper

Immerse the eggplant slices in lightly salted water for thirty minutes, then rinse and squeeze them gently. Pat dry. Spread slices on a cookie sheet and bake at 350 degrees for ten minutes. Remove from oven and allow to cool.

In a skillet, fry the ground meat and onions until well done. Add tomato sauce, herbs and spices to meat and onions. Continue to cook uncovered for about twenty minutes or until the liquid has been absorbed. Set aside mixture.

WHITE SAUCE

3 teaspoons butter
3 tablespoons flour
2 cups warm milk
¼ teaspoon ground nutmeg
¼ teaspoon pepper
¼ teaspoon salt
¾ cup grated cheddar cheese
¾ cup Parmesan cheese
2 eggs

For the white sauce, melt butter in a saucepan, stir in the flour and gradually add the warm milk, whisking to remove any lumps. Stirring constantly, bring mixture to a boil and cook until thickened. Remove saucepan from heat, and stir in the spices and cheese. Let the sauce cool. In small bowl, beat eggs with whisk. Slowly add eggs to cooled mixture. Set aside.

Use eight small individual casserole dishes or one nine-by-thirteen-inch pan (lightly coated with a nonstick cooking spray). The moussaka should be layered as follows: eggplant slices covered by potato slices, then meat sauce. Repeat these three steps. Finally, pour white sauce over the top.

Bake at 350 degrees for one hour or until top is golden brown.

(Dish can be prepared ahead of time and refrigerated.)

About the Author

Pam Hanson and Barbara Andrews are a daughter-mother writing team. They have had twenty books published together. Pam has taught journalism at Northern Arizona University and West Virginia University. Recently, she relocated to Nebraska, where she lives with her husband, also a professor, and their two sons. Barbara shares their home. Previous to their partnership, Barbara had twenty-one novels published under her own name. Currently, she writes a column and articles about collectible postcards. She is the mother of four and the grandmother of seven.